"And if I were to ask you to marry me...?"

Even as a hypothetical question it made Bianca's heart leap. But she answered quietly, "_Marriage_ isn't the magic word, Joe. _Love_ is, and I think we mean different things by it. It's not only wanting to sleep with someone. Love is more than physical attraction; it's mental, as well—a total rapport."

"Never quite total, I fancy. There must be some differences, surely?"

"Minor ones...yes, I suppose so," she conceded. "But no major gulfs."

"And you feel there are between us?" he persisted.

"Obviously. This is one of them—what we're discussing. You want to be free and uncommitted, and I—" She broke off hastily. How could she tell this man that she wanted to be loved unreservedly, passionately... and forever?

ANNE WEALE
is also the author of these

Harlequin Presents

and these

Harlequin Romances

Many of these titles are available at your local bookseller.

For a free catalogue listing all available Harlequin Romances and Harlequin Presents, send your name and address to:

HARLEQUIN READER SERVICE
1440 South Priest Drive, Tempe, AZ 85281
Canadian address: Stratford, Ontario N5A 6W2

ANNE WEALE

a touch of the devil

Harlequin Books

TORONTO · LONDON · LOS ANGELES · AMSTERDAM
SYDNEY · HAMBURG · PARIS · STOCKHOLM · ATHENS · TOKYO

Harlequin Presents edition published July 1982
ISBN 0-373-10511-8

Original hardcover edition published in 1980
by Mills & Boon Limited

CHAPTER ONE

THE first time Bianca saw him, he was sitting by himself at a table in El Delfin, eating a salad and reading a paperback. It had been a long time since she had felt the ignition of an instant physical attraction. Not since her meeting with Michael, and that was more than two years ago. Now, looking across the restaurant at the man intent on his book, she felt the same flurry of excitement as when she had first met Michael Leigh and begun a relationship which, at one time, she had hoped would lead to marriage.

Michael had been fair and grey-eyed, typically English. The man on the other side of the restaurant was black-haired and darkly tanned. A Spaniard? Somehow she didn't think so. In general the men of the Costa Blanca, which was the only part of Spain she knew well, were not especially attractive to a girl from northern Europe. Usually they were on the short side, sallow-skinned and, once past their early twenties, inclined to be overweight. Judging by the breadth of his shoulders, the man who had caught her attention stood six foot or more, without an ounce of spare flesh on his big, muscular frame.

'What shall we start with, Bianca?' asked the man with whom she was dining. 'Soup, or the special salad?'

Quickly Bianca returned her attention to the menu. 'Salad for me, I think, Peter.'

At forty-five Peter Lincoln was more than twenty years her senior. His hair was grey but still thick, and his slight but well-knit figure was that of a man who swam every day of the year and spent much of his time tending a large garden on land which, before he and Sheila had tamed it, had been part of the mountainside surrounding his luxurious villa.

Probably, to a woman nearer his age, he was still attractive. Certainly as a wealthy widower with a beautiful house and a motor cruiser on which to avoid the crowded beaches of July and August, he was a most eligible catch at whom many widows and divorcees in the expatriate community had set their caps.

To Bianca he was a friend; a nice, sad, lonely older man who had eased some of her own loneliness by infecting her with his enthusiasm for Mediterranean gardening. She had often thought that he and her mother would have been perfect for each other.

But her mother was dead and, even if she had not been struck down by the long, incurable illness which had brought Bianca to Spain to nurse her, Carla could never have become the second Mrs Peter Lincoln. Legally, if in no other way, she had been the wife of Ben Hollis, Bianca's dissolute stepfather.

As she and Peter shared a large *ensalada* garnished with asparagus and black olives, Bianca tried not to let her glance stray across the restaurant to the man sitting on his own. Since her relationship with Michael had ended in pain and disillusionment, there had been no men in her life. Indeed, apart from occasional outings with Peter, she had had no social life at all. So it was strange and unnerving suddenly to find herself intensely aware of a stranger.

Another reason why she thought he could not be a Spaniard was because it was early for anyone Spanish to be eating their evening meal. A good many of the foreigners who had come to Spain on retirement continued to rise, eat and sleep at much the same times as they had in their countries of origin. The younger foreigners, particularly those with permits to work in Spain, had of necessity to adapt themselves to local meal-times and, at night, would arrive in the restaurants as the more elderly expatriates were leaving to go home to bed.

If Bianca was right in taking the dark man for a foreigner because of his powerful build and early eating habits, perhaps he was one of the Boat People. This was how, in her mind, she designated the occupants of the many different sorts of craft berthed along the public quay of the once-small fishing port which, since Spain's tourist boom and because of its benign winter climate, had become an all-year-round haven for people from colder countries.

Unexpectedly, while she and Peter were eating their main course of pork cooked with prunes, he made it possible for her to look at the dark man again saying, 'Ah, there's the chap I met at the harbour the other day. Rather an interesting character.'

'Oh, really? In what way?' asked Bianca.

'He looks a pretty rugged customer, don't you think? And obviously he is. Until a couple of years ago, he was in the Spanish Foreign Legion—one of the very few Englishmen to serve in it, I should imagine.'

'I didn't realise Spain had a Foreign Legion.'

'Nor did I, but apparently it has and, like the French Foreign Legion, I gather it serves as a bolt-hole for a good many unsavoury types. Joe—I don't know his surname—didn't join for that reason. He enlisted when he left school, His grandparents live in southern Spain and, spending holidays with them, he picked up enough basic Spanish to see him through his training. But it must take a good deal of guts for a lad of eighteen to enlist in a foreign army—particularly in an outfit as tough as the Legion. I wish Mark had that sort of backbone.'

Mark, she knew, was Peter's rather unsatisfactory

younger son who seemed to have grown up with the idea that there was little point in his working for a living when his father could afford to keep him in idleness.

'How did you get into conversation with him?' asked Bianca, studying the strongly marked profile of the man on the opposite side of the restaurant.

What was he reading? she wondered. She could tell he was a fellow bookworm by the speed with which he turned over the pages, and the fact that even when people passed close to his table he remained undistracted.

'He's berthed his boat next to *Sheila*,' said Peter, referring to the cruiser named after his wife.

'Is he staying here for long?'

'That I don't know. He didn't say. If you'd like to meet him, I'll ask him to join us for coffee.'

'Oh, no—no, I don't want to meet him,' she answered hastily. 'But perhaps you'd like to talk to him again.' She wondered why she felt it necessary to deny her own interest.

'I'm quite satisfied with my present company,' said Peter with a smile. 'But I think it would do you good to enlarge your circle of acquaintances, and to meet someone nearer to your own age for a change. When we've had our sweet, I'll go over and have a word with him.'

However his intention was frustrated because, when he had finished his main course, the man named Joe did not order a pudding but closed his book and pushed back his chair.

On his feet he was even taller than Bianca had surmised. A line from *La Chica de Ipanema*, a South American song on one of her stepsister's records, came into her mind. When the song was sung in English, by a girl, the line was —*Tall and tanned, and young and handsome, the boy from Ipanema* ...

But the stranger who had called it to mind wasn't, strictly speaking, handsome and, although young, he wasn't a boy but a man—every lithe, superb inch of him.

Was he going to pay his bill and leave? Or was he removing to the bar, there to have coffee and his preferred *digestivo*? She had noticed that, with his meal, he had drunk only a bottle of mineral water, but she thought it very unlikely that any ex-legionnaire would be a teetotaller.

To her surprise, instead of doing either of the things she had expected, he went to the upright piano not far from where he had been sitting and placed his book on the top of it. Then he opened the lid and sat down, and began to play.

Bianca knew that, on the far side of the bar, there was a dark smoke-stuffy disco which didn't open until later and where, on Saturdays and Sundays, a small live group replaced the taped pop music to which local and visiting teenagers danced on weekdays. But on the few occasions when Peter had brought her to El Delfin there had never been music in the restaurant, although there had always been a piano there.

'What do you think of my new pianist?' enquired the Dutch owner of the place when, about ten minutes later, he made his customary tour of the tables, speaking briefly to new customers and at greater length to his regulars.

Since the death of his wife, Peter had taken to eating out three or four times a week. Bianca would have liked to invite him to Casa Mimosa more often, but he could not stand Ben. Sheila Lincoln and another woman had been killed in a collision with a drunken driver on their way home after a shopping trip to Alicante, the nearest big city. Ben didn't drive, but it was no secret that he often drank more than was good for him and, since the loss of his wife, Peter's casual contempt for heavy drinkers had become a fierce detestation. In his opinion, Bianca was foolish to put herself out for her step-relations. He thought she should go back to England and resume her career and her life there. He did not know about the break-up with Michael whom, if she returned, she would, inevitably, meet again.

'He's good,' replied Peter, in answer to the Dutchman's question. 'I like background music, provided it *is* in the background and doesn't drown one's conversation.'

'Have you engaged him for the summer?' asked Bianca.

The Dutchman shook his head. 'I can't persuade him to sign a contract for any definite period, but he says he may stay for some time. I think he's one of the roving kind ... doesn't like to be tied down.' He glanced over his shoulder at the man whose well-shaped brown hands were moving lazily over the keyboard. 'This kind of music suits our early diners, but later he plays in the disco, and he's an excellent jazz pianist. You should stay and hear him.'

Peter shook his head. 'I'm an early riser, and don't like burning the candle at both ends. By eleven I'm ready for bed.'

'I am the opposite. I go to bed in the small hours, and I don't get up before eleven in the morning. Your way is more healthy, I think,' said the Dutchman, with a rueful shrug.

Before he moved on to another table, he smiled at Bianca and she sensed he was curious about her. He might know that she was the stepdaughter of the English artist who spent more time drinking than painting. Probably what he was pondering was her relationship with Peter. On more than one occasion when they had dined together she had been aware of speculative glances and murmured comments. Many of the older members of the foreign community had nothing better to do with their time than to pass on the latest rumours and titbits of scandal. It was foolish to care what they thought, and yet she couldn't help being irked at being taken for Peter's girl-friend when she was not.

In the modern meaning of the term, she had never been anyone's girl-friend—not even Michael's. Sometimes she wondered if it was because she had not slept with him that she had lost him. At first, when he had written to tell her he had found someone else, she had regretted bitterly that her memories of him did not include making love in the fullest sense. In the first and worst stage of her anguish, when it seemed that her heart was broken and she would never love again, part of her torment had been that now she would never experience passion at its zenith. But later, as she came to realise that Michael was not the great love of her life, she was glad she had stuck to her principles, even if they were unfashionable.

She watched an elderly man get up from his table and go across to the pianist in whose ear he murmured what she guessed to be a request for a favourite tune. The man called Joe nodded his head and, when he had finished the number he was playing, began to play Irving Berlin's *How Many Times Must I Say I Love You.* Bianca saw that the man who had asked for it was holding his wife's hand and smiling at her. Perhaps they were celebrating the anniversary of their wedding. It might even, judging by their appearance, be their golden wedding anniversary, and yet they were gazing at each other as fondly as a pair of young lovers.

That's what I want, thought Bianca. The kind of love which lasts a lifetime, not just for six months or a year.

Her gaze returned to the pianist whose thick black hair had the sheen of a raven's wing in the light from the lamp on top of the piano. Were his eyes also gypsy-dark? She had yet to see him full face.

On impulse, she said to Peter, 'Excuse me a moment,' and rose from the table to cross the room to the door with the discreet silhouette of a woman applying lipstick.

There was no one else in the powder room, and she sat down on a stool and put her bag on the counter beneath one of the four oval mirrors. The glass reflected a slim girl with sun-streaked brown hair and large, rather serious grey eyes. She was not a beauty like her mother, nor had she the pin-up prettiness of Lucy, her unruly stepsister; but Bianca had never been seriously dissatisfied with her looks. She was content with her assets which were a good skin and good teeth, and a long neck and pleasant voice. Her defects she accepted philosophically.

Fortunately she had inherited her mother's eye for colour, and also Carla's flair for wearing cheap clothes with an expensive effect. Tonight she had put on a pale green suede-look overdress with a darker green shirt, both from chain stores in Oxford Street. But the crêpe-de-chine scarf round her throat had been made in Italy for Jaeger, and this one extravagant item made her outfit look as if it might have come from some expensive boutique in Knightsbridge or Alicante.

After spending a few moments repairing her lipstick and flicking a comb through the gamine haircut which was dry within ten minutes of a daily shampoo under the shower, she stood up, conscious of butterflies fluttering inside her. Seen at close quarters, would the ex-legionnaire be disappointing? Eyes too small, or too close together? Mouth weaker than it looked in profile? And even if a closer view did not dissolve the attraction she had felt on first catching sight of him, would it be mutual? She might not be his type. A big man himself, he might only go for a girl with a much more voluptuous figure than hers.

When she re-entered the restaurant, the pianist was looking at the keyboard and it was not until she paused by the side of the piano that he glanced up and met her eyes. His were not dark but hazel. Against the deep tan of his skin they looked almost golden.

'W-would you play something for me?'

'With pleasure ... if I know it.' His voice matched his physique and his hair; a dark brown voice, quiet in tone and, a little to her surprise, without any regional accent.

'*A Man And A Woman.*' Although the romantic theme music had long been a favourite with her, suddenly she wished she had asked for a tune with a more impersonal title.

He was smiling at her now, the hazel eyes swiftly appraising her, and then unequivocally signalling that he liked what he saw as much as she did.

'*A Man And A Woman,*' he repeated, and never in her life—not with Michael or with any other man—had Bianca felt so intensely aware of being a female confronting an intensely masculine male.

When he said, 'Yes, I know it,' she murmured her thanks and hurried back to the table where, to her relief, she had a few minutes to recover from the impact of Joe's personality—or would sexuality have been more accurate?—because in her absence Peter had gone to the men's room.

All the time her request was being played, she kept her eyes on the flowers decorating the table, but in her mind's eye she was seeing the strong-featured, rawboned brown face, and the hazel eyes glinting the message that she *was* his type—very much so.

When the music ended she clapped, as the golden wedding couple had, and Joe looked over his shoulder to where she was sitting, still alone, and smiled. Then instead of continuing to play, he rose and came to her table. He moved with the supple grace of a panther, she thought;

having, like a panther, immense reserves of muscle power.

'I'm taking a break for ten minutes. May I buy you a drink or'—eyeing the other empty coffee cup—'would that be trespassing?'

'Not at all. Won't you sit down?'

'Thank you.' He beckoned to one of the waiters, seated himself in the chair next to hers, and said, 'I'm Joe Crawford.'

She was about to tell him her name when Peter reappeared, and instead she said, 'I believe you two have met before.'

Joe rose to shake hands and exchange a greeting with the older man. Then the waiter arrived and he ordered drinks. Peter, who had had half a bottle of wine with his meal, and a Spanish brandy with his coffee, asked for another *café con leche*. Bianca, who seldom drank spirits, asked for another glass of the house wine, and Joe ordered beer for himself. The image of an ex-legionnaire tossing back hard liquor the way other people drank orange juice didn't, as yet, seem to apply to him.

As the two men reseated themselves, she saw him glance at her left hand on which the only ring was a twist of silver studded with tiny green beads which she wore on her little finger.

Clearly he was debating her relationship to Peter. Surely he wouldn't jump to the wrong conclusion? The fact that she had invited him to sit down should disabuse him of the idea that she and Peter were close friends in the gossip-column sense. For surely no girl with an older man in tow would encourage a young man to muscle in?

'Playing the piano seems a fairly rare accomplishment nowadays,' said Peter. 'How did you come by it?'

'My grandmother taught me the rudiments, and I found I could play tunes by ear. I had some lessons at school, but

I wasn't interested in the hours of practice needed to become professional. But any competent strummer can pick up a living round the Mediterranean.'

'You don't play any instrument, do you, Bianca?' asked Peter.

She shook her head. 'I like music, as a listener, but I have a very poor ear.'

'Are you English?' Joe asked her.

Surprised, she said, 'Yes. Don't I look it?'

'You do, but your name is Italian, and I've never known an English girl called Bianca before.'

'My mother had some Italian blood in her, and my parents were living in Italy when I was born. But my surname couldn't be more English. It's Dawson.'

She wished he would ask her what she was doing in Spain so that she could explain her presence there, and add some remark about Peter being a friend of the family. But he turned to Peter and began talking about the facilities of the harbour, and she felt in her bones that he *had* jumped to the wrong conclusion about them. The current of magnetism which had vibrated between them now had been switched off at his end of the line. Although he glanced at her sometimes in the course of conversation, the golden lion's eyes under the mobile dark eyebrows no longer held the gleam which had been in them when first he saw her, and when he came to her table. Now he was polite but indifferent, whereas she was still pulse-quickeningly conscious that under the table his long muscular thigh must be within centimetres of hers and, on the table, he had only to move his elbow a fraction for his sinewy forearm to brush against her softer arm. His naturally splendid proportions, and the super-fitness of his condition—a legacy of his Legion service, presumably—made

Peter, who was in good shape for his age, seem puny by comparison.

Joe drank his beer fast, and rose. 'I must get back to work. Is there anything else you'd like me to play for you?'

He addressed the question to them both, and Peter said, 'How about *Night and Day*?'

'Surely.' With a civil nod he turned away, and was soon back at his place at the piano.

'I gather he's already played one request for you?' said Peter.

'Yes.'

'I should think from a woman's point of view he's an attractive fellow, but perhaps a bit of a ne'er-do-well.'

'Why do you say that? When you were talking about him earlier, you said you wished Mark had his backbone.'

'In some ways, yes. But I shouldn't care to see Mark living the vagabond life which this young chap appears to lead. Though at least he's supporting himself, and not relying on State hand-outs as some of Mark's cronies do. But Joe seems intelligent enough to do something better than this with his life. Playing in bars may cover his expenses, but I doubt if it would support a wife and children.'

'Perhaps he doesn't want a wife and children. People don't settle down as early as they used to.'

'No, and I'm all in favour of young people seeing more of the world than many of my generation did,' agreed Peter. 'But the fact remains that youth doesn't last for ever, and sooner or later we all have to pull our weight and become useful members of the community.'

It was a view he had aired many times and on which, given a willing listener, he would expound at length. He was inclined to sermonise. More than once Lucy had embarrassed Bianca by showing and even expressing her boredom. Bianca herself was sometimes bored, but she did her best to conceal it. Listening to Peter's homilies was a small price to pay for his many kindnesses, and his sympathetic ear for her problems.

While she was listening to him, and saying Yes and No at suitable moments, she noticed a waiter place a glass of beer on top of the piano and indicate to Joe that it had been ordered for him by the golden wedding couple.

Without interrupting his playing, Joe bowed his thanks to them. He said something to the waiter. Immediately the man looked across the restaurant at her and at Peter. As clearly as if she had overheard the question, she knew Joe had asked the *camarero* who they were. In reply the man gave a shrug, and she saw his lips form '*No se.*' An instant later he grinned and said something else in a manner which made her certain that although he couldn't give any reliable information, he was prepared to make a bawdy surmise as to why a girl of her age was dining *à deux* with a man who was not, but was old enough to be, her father.

For some seconds she felt so annoyed that, almost, she jumped up and went over to make it clear to Joe that Peter was neither her lover nor her protector, but a widower still grieving for his wife, and definitely not the type to lust after girls half his age.

But then she decided that if Joe was the kind of person who, without proof, was prepared to believe the worst of people, she did not want to further his acquaintance anyway.

Soon afterwards they left the restaurant, and Peter drove her home to the small villa, not far from his larger one, bought by her father ten years earlier as a holiday house and an investment.

Both villas were in an area where residents had the advantage of remaining comparatively unscathed by the hurly-burly of the tourist season. But there were also disadvantages, particularly for a family whose only transport was the moped on which Lucy went back and forth to her job in an estate agent's office.

If Bianca wanted to go to town, she was dependent on an infrequent bus service, or lifts from friendly motorists; and sometimes the motorists became too friendly. More than once some retired empire-builder or Colonel Blimp whom she would have thought past such urges had started patting her leg, or attempted to press a brandy-smelling kiss upon her reluctant lips. Unless it was absolutely necessary, she seldom went farther than the village for her household shopping. But now that spring had arrived—although throughout the province of Alicante much of the winter was spring-like, hence the sign at the provincial border, *La casa de la primavera*—she was thinking of buying a bicycle to enable her to pedal to the sea in which she enjoyed swimming more than in Peter's chlorinated, solar-heated pool.

They returned to Casa Mimosa to find the place ablaze with light but no one there. Doubtless Ben was drinking in the village bar, and presumably Lucy had gone to one of the discos.

After saying goodnight to Peter, Bianca went round the house switching off most of the lights.

By now she was resigned to the fact that appealing to Ben and his daughter to try to economise was a waste of breath. Sometimes she was tempted to take Peter's advice and leave them to manage on their own. Always two factors restrained her from packing her bags. One was that her mother had begged her to stay with Lucy until she had learned more sense than she had at present; the other was that, like Carla before her, Bianca loved Spain and felt it was her spiritual home. The rugged grandeur of the mountains, the terraced foothills and vineyards, the colourful displays of fish and fruit on the stalls in the small-town markets, the friendliness and animation of the people and, above all, the invigorating climate made her long to be able to live there in happy tranquillity, unencumbered by her present responsibilities.

Why, after six years of widowhood, Carla had married Ben Hollis was a mystery to her daughter. Except that they were both artists—Carla an outstandingly gifted painter of still life whose pictures commanded high prices in a leading London gallery, and Ben a hack who churned out garish souvenirs of Spain for the tourist trade—they had had nothing in common. But not by so much as a sigh had Carla ever conceded that her second marriage was a disaster. Loyalty and courage had been as integral to her character as her ebullient sense of humour. It was her laughter which Bianca missed most, for neither Lucy nor Ben had much humour in them, nor had Peter. They never fell about laughing at some absurd joke as Carla and Bianca had often done, and as Joe Crawford looked as if he might.

Thinking about him as she lay in bed waiting to hear the shambling footsteps which would indicate that Ben was again in his cups, she knew she ought not to let her mind dwell on a man who could only become an additional complication in an already complicated life. Probably she would never see him again. By the next time Peter took her to El Delfin, it was more than likely that Joe would have moved on. Firmly, she dismissed him from her thoughts.

CHAPTER TWO

NOT far from the Casa Mimosa and behind Peter's house,
Bellavista, there was a mountain criss-crossed by narrow
mule tracks, most of which Bianca had followed many times
since first coming to Spain as a teenager.

In summer it was too hot to go for long walks, but often
on winter holidays she would put on an old pair of jeans to
protect her legs from the gorse, and fill a dark leather *bota*
bought by her father with sparkling mineral water, and
disappear up the mountain for three or four hours.

One of her favourite places was near a derelict *casa* built
on one of the highest terraces. She would sit on the top of
a drystone wall, some of which were said to have been built
in the time of the Moors, and dangle her legs and gaze at
the distant sierras, dreaming impossible dreams of having
the Casa Mimosa—named after the beautiful tree which in
January dominated the garden with its mass of fluffy yellow
flowers—to herself.

It was on what she thought likely to be her last walk for
some months that she had an accident. Normally she was
as sure-footed as the mules and donkeys which, although
Spanish agriculture was becoming increasingly mechanised,
were still sometimes to be seen on the mountainside or
pulling carts along the tarred roads. But on this occasion
she had scarcely begun her descent when she trod on a
loose piece of rock which gave way beneath her. With a
startled exclamation which became an indrawn gasp of
pain, she fell and twisted her ankle.

That it was no mere wrench but a severe sprain was soon

apparent from the swelling. There was still some water in the *bota*. Unscrewing the mouthpiece which enabled a practised user to direct a thin jet of liquid between his or her parted lips, she soaked her cotton headscarf and bound it round her thickened ankle in the hope that it would enable her to hobble home. But she soon found this was impossible and, as bad luck would have it, she was stranded on a stretch of the path which was out of sight of the houses far below. So even if she yelled for help, and was heard, she could not signal her position and, because of the peculiar sound effects caused by the steep bluffs above her, she might sound far from where she was.

'Oh, *hell*!' she exclaimed aloud.

Unlike Lucy, who seemed to think it sophisticated to lard her conversation with all the crudest expletives, Bianca was more restrained. Sometimes she wondered if there were any men left who, like her father, never swore in front of women. Certainly Michael had not moderated his language for her benefit, and seemed to have been unaware that certain words made her flinch, inwardly if not outwardly. It had been one of the many differences between them which, at the time, she had tried to pretend were only trivial but which, later, she recognised as the small but not unimportant disharmonies on which a marriage could founder. At heart she was an old-fashioned girl who needed an old-fashioned man, the kind who instinctively protected and cherished all women, and particularly one who belonged to him. She didn't want to be equal: she wanted to be complementary.

But although these reflections had been in her mind before her mishap, afterwards the pain of her injury drove out all thoughts other than how to get down to road level.

It was then that, from higher up, she heard someone whistling. She knew it was not the *pastor* who grazed his sheep on the plateau at the top of the mountain. Had it been he, she would have heard also the tonkle-tonkle of the sheep's bells. It must therefore be someone using the mule-track as a short cut from the town on the other side of the mountain. With a sigh of relief she waited for him to appear. No sound had ever been more welcome than the clear whistled notes of what, as the walker came closer, she recognised as one of her favourite pieces of music, Tchaikovsky's only violin concerto.

Somehow this gave her the feeling that whoever was coming was not a Spaniard. She hoped he would not be too elderly. At worst he would be able to fetch help and, if he had the energy for mountain-walking, probably, whatever his age, he would be able to assist her himself.

As it turned out, the man of whom her first glimpse was his head and shoulders beyond a large clump of wild rosemary was, in one way, an ideal person to rescue her. Nevertheless her relief at seeing Joe Crawford coming towards her was mixed with a certain dismay. In the interval since their first meeting, she had found it difficult to forget him. A second encounter could only make it more difficult.

She was sitting in a position which, when Joe first saw her, made him think she was merely resting. He stopped his whistling, and smiled—the same smile he had given her when she paused by the piano, before Peter's presence had made a change in his manner.

'Good afternoon,' he said pleasantly. 'Are you on your way up or down?'

'I *was* going down until I slipped. I've hurt my ankle ... sprained it. I'm sorry to be a nuisance, but I wonder if you could lend me your arm to get down?'

'Of course. Let me have a look.' He went down on his haunches beside her and gently unpeeled the improvised bandage.

Bianca had noticed before that, unlike those of some big, tall men, his hands were not thick-fingered hams, nor had he the short, stubby fingers to be found on a good many pianists. Broad at the knuckles, and obviously those of a man whose life style included a good deal of manual work, his hands looked both strong and deft. She could imagine them folding into punishing fists, or caressing a woman as gently as a ripple on the sand.

'Phew! *Pobrecita!*' he murmured, when he saw the extent of the swelling.

She knew it meant 'Poor little one', and it sent a curious thrill through her.

Then he said, 'You'll have to grit your teeth for a moment or two, I'm afraid. This could be a break and, if it is, you'll need to be brought down by stretcher. If not, I can carry you down, although it will be damned uncomfortable.'

Afterwards, she knew it was a measure of his effect on her that although what he did to test the severity of the injury was, as he had warned her, fairly agonising, the pain was partly anaesthetised by her response to his nearness.

He was stripped to the waist, his cotton-knit shirt pulled carelessly through his belt, a black leather one ornamented with fifteen or twenty of the pierced silver-coloured Spanish coins, now not often seen, worth fifty *centimos* or half a *peseta*. His shoulders and chest were as tanned as his lean, dark face; the skin like brown silk over the strong bones and muscles. In his two years out of the Legion, he did not appear to have lost his commando-fitness.

'Hm, only a sprain—but a bad one. You won't walk on that for some time.' He re-wetted and replaced the scarf. Then he stood up and looked down at her, the golden eyes slightly quizzical. 'Now, if you're under the impression that I'm going to carry you down in the manner of a Hollywood hero, I'm afraid you'll have to forget it. There are only two ways to get down a track as rough as this one—by fireman's lift, which is not for any distance, or by piggyback. If I were you, I'd have a swig of this before we start.'

From the pocket at the back of his trousers he produced an old-fashioned hip flask of leather and silver, unscrewed the cap, and offered it to her.

'What is it?' Bianca asked doubtfully.

'Spanish brandy. To be precise, Fundador. It may not be your preferred brand, but it should help to dull the jolts.'

'I don't much like brandy.'

Again he went down on his haunches. 'If you were my girl, you'd learn to like it. There are circumstances in which a shared glass of brandy is the perfect conclusion.'

He could only mean after love, she thought, in startled confusion; and she had a sudden clear picture of herself reclining on a bed with her head on his shoulder and her body languid from pleasure, while they talked and alternately sipped from a large glass of brandy.

It was such an intimate vision to have of herself and of him—almost a stranger—that it sent a hot wave of colour flooding from her neck to her forehead. In an effort to hide her embarrassment, she almost snatched at the hip flask and gulped down a mouthful of what, to her unaccustomed palate, seemed like liquid fire.

'Easy, girl! We don't want you tipsy.' He took the flask from her and replaced the stopper. 'My back may be sweaty from climbing. I'd better put this on'—pulling his shirt free of his belt.

A few minutes later they were on their way down the mountain, Bianca's arms round his neck and her legs astride his hard waist.

The trip down *was* damned uncomfortable. The dangling position of her foot made the blood course painfully through the distended tissues. And, light on his feet as he was, with the easy gait of a man well used to rough ground, Joe could not avoid sometimes jolting her. But again the discomfort was not what she was to remember, but rather the clean male smell of his crisp dark hair and brown neck.

At the foot of the track where it joined a macadamed road through an area of pinewoods and undeveloped building plots, he set her carefully down.

'Now for the Hollywood bit,' he announced, with a teasing gleam. And before Bianca had grasped what he was about, he had her up in his arms, like a bride being carried over the threshold, and was striding the rest of the way with her.

'I must say you're not short of grit,' he said, some yards further on. 'Your foot must be giving you hell, but you haven't made a murmur.'

'Oh, it could be worse,' she said lightly, inordinately pleased by his praise. 'What luck you came by—I could have been stuck there for ages.'

'Don't you carry a whistle? You should. Any girl who walks on her own in places where there's some risk of having an accident should have a good whistle on her. It's ten times easier than shouting.'

'Yes, I suppose it must be. I hadn't thought of it. I'll get one—although now it's almost the end of the walking season.'

'What's your summer exercise? Swimming? Tennis? Sailing?'

'I swim, and sometimes I snorkel. I don't play tennis, or sail. I've never been on a sailing boat, only on motor cruisers.'

'There's no comparison,' he said. 'A motor cruiser is far too noisy and smelly. For me, the whole point of a boat is to get away from the racket going on ashore. Which way?'

this as they came to a fork in the road.

'Left, please.' She wondered if Ben would be at home.

It did not trouble her that he might have been drinking. It was not her fault that she had a sot for a stepfather. But she did mind him seeing Joe, and probably taunting her about him. Ben had a malicious streak in him. If he guessed the effect Joe had on her, it would divert him to twit her. Lucy, too, would enjoy goading her. She had never liked Carla but had not dared to be rude to her because—to do him justice—her father would not have stood for it. He had loved Carla, in his weak way. But Lucy had no such compunction in being offensive to Bianca, knowing that, in any quarrel between them, Ben would take her part against his stepdaughter.

Nevertheless, although she would have chosen to avoid an encounter with Ben, it was with greater dismay that, as they approached Bellavista, she saw Peter driving home in his silver Mercedes.

He stopped it outside his gates, and leapt out, looking concerned at the sight of Bianca in Joe's arms.

'It's only a sprained ankle, Peter,' she said, as he hurried towards them.

'Good God! How did it happen? You can give her to me now,' holding out his arms to take her.

'She's no feather,' was Joe's response and, although he might not have meant to impugn the older man's strength, that was obviously how Peter took it.

A flush of annoyance tinged his already florid complexion. He said curtly, 'Bring her into the house, and I'll call a doctor.'

He was one of the few British residents to have a telephone, which he needed in order to keep in touch with his broker in London.

Bianca opened her mouth to protest, but was interrupted

by Joe, who said, 'Oh, I don't think that's necessary. If you have a decent first aid kit, I can patch her up.'

'Have you been trained in first aid?' Peter asked sharply.

'Well enough to deal with an injury a good deal more serious than a sprained ankle,' was Joe's answer.

And before Bianca could say that she would rather go home, she was being carried up the steps to the spacious veranda of Peter's six-bedroomed villa where, before the death of his wife, they had entertained friends from England and given large, lavish parties.

'If you go inside and call Juanita, she'll give you the first aid box,' Peter instructed peremptorily, as Joe laid her carefully on a sofa.

He spoke in the tone which Bianca imagined that ill-bred people had used to servants in the days when they could ride rough-shod with their employees. She could not understand his antipathetic attitude to the man but for whom she would still be stranded on the mountain.

She saw Joe raise a sardonic eyebrow, but he kept silent and did as Peter had ordered.

'Peter, wasn't that rather ... high-handed?' she suggested, when he had left them.

The sofa was a large four-seater with ample room for him to sit down beside her. He did so, and answered, 'I don't like that young man. He's too cocky by half.'

'Cocky?' she exclaimed, in amazement. Self-assured, yes. But not cocky. 'You liked him before,' she said blankly.

'I don't now,' was his abrupt retort. 'What were you doing up on the mountain with him? Don't you think it's unwise to go up there with a man you don't know from Adam? The fellow might get out of hand. He looks the type.'

The animosity in his tone astounded her. She had never known him to speak so bitingly of anyone. She had always believed Peter to be an exceptionally tolerant man.

'I wasn't on the mountain *with* him. I was walking, and he was walking, and fortunately for me he appeared on the scene a short time after I'd hurt myself. I can't understand why you've suddenly taken a dislike to him. If you've heard something nasty about him, more than likely it's unfounded gossip. You know how people talk here. They repeat the most scandalous rumours.'

'It's not what I've heard, it's what my instinct tells me. For a girl of your age, you're not very worldly, Bianca. In fact you're refreshingly innocent. I've noticed your reaction if someone tells an off-colour joke, or some randy old fool has too much to drink at a party and tries to paw you.'

'What has that to do with Joe?'

'If he made a pass at you, you might not be able to deal with him. No doubt most of the women he's known have been a promiscuous lot. Whores very likely, half of them.'

'Peter!' she uttered, dumbfounded.

'You see? You're shocked. It wouldn't even occur to you that a man who's been in a rough, tough mob like the Legion—some of them gaol-birds and thugs—is unlikely to be too fastidious about the women he sleeps with.'

'No, it wouldn't,' she answered indignantly. 'Not when the man is like Joe—well-mannered, obviously educated.'

'That could be only a veneer. Neville Heath was as suave as they come. He had the charm of the devil—and he was a devil, a murderer.'

'You're not suggesting that Joe——' She broke off, beginning to wonder if Peter's extraordinary behaviour was a symptom of some kind of breakdown, perhaps a delayed reaction to the loss of his wife.

She put her hand on his arm and said soothingly, 'Perhaps you're right, but don't worry about it. It was a chance meeting, Peter, and in the circumstances a lucky one.'

He laid his hand over hers and pressed it against his forearm. 'Perhaps I needn't in this case, but I do worry about you, my dear. You're having a rotten time as an unpaid and unthanked housekeeper to Ben and Lucy. Why should she enjoy life at your expense? Let her look after her father—and let me look after you.' He paused, obviously in the grip of strong emotion. 'I know you don't love me, but we have so much in common, and that's the best basis for marriage.'

'*Marriage?*' she echoed faintly.

Not for an instant had it struck her that his change of attitude to Joe could have been brought about by jealousy. The idea of Peter wanting to marry her was as shattering as if he had announced his intention of marrying Juanita, his Spanish daily help.

'I'm sorry to intrude, but I think you should defer your proposal until Bianca's ankle has been attended to,' said a dry voice from behind them. 'Would you mind moving, Mr Lincoln.'

Peter rose from beside her, a scowl of mingled embarrassment and annoyance on his face. Joe put the first aid box in the place where the older man had been sitting, and began to deal with the ankle by binding it with a crêpe bandage. He did it as expertly as a medical orderly, and such slight discomfort as it caused Bianca was nothing compared with her mental turmoil. She found her predominant emotion was a strong desire to tell Joe that Peter's declaration had come straight out of the blue; that she had done nothing to encourage him to propose to her, and was horrified that he had.

But as long as Peter was present, hovering anxiously behind the sofa, watching Joe in the manner of a suspicious duenna who would not be surprised to catch him attempting some stealthy impropriety, she could only keep silent.

Once, and only once, did Joe glance at her, and then with a gleam in his eyes and a quirk at the corner of his mouth which made her feel sure that he thought the reverse of the truth; that Peter's proposal was something she had engineered and would accept eagerly, as soon as he left them alone together.

'There you are,' he said, when he had finished. 'I'll be on my way. *Adiós.*'

He had walked to the edge of the veranda when she said his name and he checked and looked over his shoulder.

'Thank you ... thank you very much.'

He shrugged, and said lightly, '*De nada,*' which was the Spanish equivalent of 'You're welcome ... it was nothing.'

'Before you go, would you do one more thing for me?' Bianca asked tentatively.

'What is it?'

She couldn't be sure how much he had overheard. If he had heard only Peter's proposal, and not his reference to Ben and Lucy, Joe might be under the misapprehension that she was already a member of Peter's ménage.

She said, 'I'm beginning to feel rather exhausted. I'd like to go home. It's only just down the road if you wouldn't mind helping me to go a little further.'

'I think that's Mr Lincoln's prerogative.'

He walked away, leaving her feeling rebuffed and miserable, and in no mood to deal with a repetition of Peter's astounding offer of marriage.

To her relief, Peter seemed to have recovered some of his normal self-control. As soon as Joe was out of earshot he said, in a much calmer tone, 'I'm sorry, Bianca. I chose a bad moment to tell you how warmly I've come to feel about you. You're in pain, and probably suffering from a slight degree of shock. You should be in bed—I'll take you home immediately. Juanita must come with us to help make you comfortable.'

So it was that her last sight of Joe was as he and the silver Mercedes reached the entrance to the Casa Mimosa at the same moment, and he checked his long stride to allow the luxurious two-seater—Juanita was following on foot—to turn into the driveway.

Bianca gave him an uncertain smile, and received in return a sardonic grin with no warmth in it, only mockery. By the time Peter had stopped the car and hurried round the bonnet to help her out, the tall, erect figure of the ex-legionnaire had disappeared in the direction of the main road.

It was not until the following day that Peter repeated his proposal. By then, although her night's rest had been somewhat fitful, partly because of her throbbing ankle and partly because of her state of mind, Bianca felt more equal to the task of tactfully refusing him.

Unfortunately he would not accept that her refusal was final, and said he would ask her again when she had had more time to consider the matter.

It was not until he kissed her on the lips—not with passion, indeed very restrainedly—that she made the uncomfortable discovery that although she had liked him well enough as a friend of the family, as a prospective lover she found him almost as repulsive as the elderly lechers to whom he himself had referred the day before.

That he offered her every luxury meant nothing to Bianca. Old-fashioned in certain ways, but modern in others, she had never thought of marriage as a meal-ticket.

After leaving school she had taken a secretarial course with no special end in view until, quite by chance, she had found that research was her métier. For the past three years she had been employed as an assistant to a genealogist who made an excellent living by tracing the family trees of wealthy Australians and Americans.

This was how she had met Michael Leigh. She had been working in the Rolls Room at the Public Record Office in London, and had looked up from a pile of dusty documents, two centuries old, to find herself being watched by an attractive man on the other side of the table.

A writer who made his bread and butter working on television documentaries, but who hoped one day to become a full-time biographer, Michael had been researching the life of a Victorian field-marshal. For a time, physical attraction and community of interest professionally had misled her into thinking she loved him.

That he had chosen to follow the most insecure of livelihoods, with the possible exception of acting, had seemed as irrelevant to her as was Peter's wealth. Accustomed to supporting herself, she would have been happy to continue. She had asked of him nothing but love and the bond of marriage—not to make living together respectable, or to give her a legal claim on him, but only as a warrant that he loved her, and believed he would always love her.

To her, love was total commitment without reservations. She could not live with a man on an experimental basis.

'If we aren't sure now, at the beginning, we'll never be sure,' she had told him. 'I don't want a dummy-run, Michael. I want for better, for worse ... and if you don't feel the same way, I think we'd better say goodbye.'

Not that they had said goodbye. The impasse between them had continued until a telegram from Ben had summoned her to Spain, and Michael's farewell embrace had made her believe that perhaps her absence would prove to him that he was as committed as she. Instead of which, six weeks later, he had written to say there was someone else.

Now, looking back, she knew that Michael had been right never to say to her, 'Marry me.' They had not truly loved each other and, having made one mistake, she was nervous of making another.

It was this fear which restrained her, once her ankle was better, from going to the harbour where Joe's boat was berthed and making it clear to him that she was free, that she liked him, and that it was up to him to take things from there.

Twice, when she could walk without limping, she got as far as catching the bus to town with a pot of home-made jam in her basket as a thank-you present for his help on the day of the accident. But, each time, arriving in town, her courage had failed her. Surely, had he been as strongly attracted to her as she to him, regardless of her possible involvement with another man, Joe would have sought her out?

A month passed. Although, in addition to a good deal of domestic conflict, Bianca now dreaded the moment when Peter would again speak of marriage, there were hours at a stretch—sometimes days—when the glorious golden weather made her forget all her problems.

While some people wilted in the heat, she bloomed like the bougainvillaeas cascading over the courtyard and the vivid geraniums and pelargoniums which her mother had planted in graceful, green-glazed Spanish pots and set round the edge of the terrace.

What she particularly enjoyed was to rise at first light and pedal, on her newly acquired second-hand bike, the six kilometres to the coast, there to bathe and later to breakfast on pâté and bread still warm from the oven. She swam in Peter's free-form pool as seldom as possible, and made excuses when he asked her to dine with him.

Although Ben raised no objection to his daughter being out long past midnight, and told Bianca not to fuss, she could not help feeling that it was unwise for a girl of seventeen to be out on the town until all hours, and dependent on lifts to get home. So far nothing unpleasant had happened to Lucy, but her clothes and make-up, and her air of knowing all the answers, seemed calculated to land her in trouble eventually.

One night Bianca was reading in bed when she heard a car stop at the gate, followed by some kind of angry altercation. Before her attention was fully detached from her book, the exchange in the roadway had ended and Lucy's high heels were clicking rapidly up the path while her escort's car drew away.

It was not particularly late, only a little after midnight, but Bianca had a strong intuition that something untoward had happened. She was wearing a cotton voile nightdress which she would remove before sleeping as she found a sheet enough covering during the night. Swinging her legs over the side of the bed, she slipped her feet into mules and opened her door to find the hall still in darkness although she had heard the front door open and close. When she switched on the light, her stepsister was leaning against the door, her chest heaving with sobs and her cheeks shiny with tears.

'Lucy dear, what is it? What's happened?' Bianca went to her with open arms.

At the sight of her stepsister's distress, she forgot all Lucy's faults—the slatternly state of her bedroom, and her frequent selfishness and rudeness—and felt only concern and compassion. After all, the younger girl was the product of a broken marriage, with a father who set her a poor example. Trying as she could be, one had to make certain allowances. She was still very young, and might yet turn out well.

At first she was too hysterical for Bianca to make much sense of what had happened to her. But gradually, as she became a little more coherent, a picture emerged of precisely the kind of misadventure which the older girl had feared would befall her. On the way home, her escort had driven the car off the road to a secluded stop where he had made a pass at her. She had managed to fight him off, but it sounded as if she had been extremely lucky not to have been raped.

Lucy was deeply asleep when her stepsister left her, but it was a long time before Bianca could sleep. She could only hope that Lucy's frightening experience would prove to have been a salutary one. Had Ben been a proper father, she would have told him what had happened and left him to deal with the man who had molested his daughter. Who he was, she didn't yet know, and perhaps Lucy didn't either. He might not be one of her regular partners at the discos, but a newcomer on the local scene—perhaps someone merely passing through.

Whoever he was, Bianca doubted if Ben had the guts to tackle him, or sufficient command of Spanish. Lucy spoke it fluently but, after years in the country, Ben had only a smattering of the language, not as much as Bianca had picked up in the nine months since her arrival.

In the morning Lucy had a pounding headache which confirmed Bianca's suspicion that alcohol had contributed to her condition the night before. The girl felt too seedy to go to work, and her stepsister decided to take the opportunity of using the moped, which had two capacious panniers, and going to the open-air market held once a week near the harbour.

'Lucy, was it a Spaniard or a foreigner who drove you

home last night?' she asked. 'Whoever it was, I don't think
he should be allowed to get off scot-free. I don't feel a complaint to the Guardia would serve any purpose, and it
might be unpleasant for you. But if he's a young man, we
could complain to his family.'

For a moment Lucy hesitated. Then, somewhat reluc-
tantly, she said, 'He was English, and he hasn't any family.
He bums around on his own.'

'Do you mean he's one of the hippies?' Bianca asked, in
surprise.

There were one or two hippy communities in that part of
Spain, but she had never heard of any of them owning a
car—they appeared to hitch everywhere—nor, from what
she knew of their way of life, would she have expected any
of the men to force himself on a woman. She regarded
them as shiftless types, and often slovenly in their appearance, but also she gave them credit for being gentle people,
not given to violence of any kind.

'No, he lives on a boat,' Lucy answered, 'and plays the
piano at El Delfin.'

'What? I don't believe it!' Bianca gasped.

'What d'you mean? You don't know him, do you?'

It was Bianca's turn to hesitate. 'No ... no, not really.
I've spoken to him. Peter has met him, and I saw him
playing when we dined there. He seemed a ... a very nice
man.'

'Well, he isn't,' said Lucy angrily. 'He's a beast ... a
swine. I can't stand him. Do shut up about it, Bianca. I
don't want to talk or think about it.' With which she
slumped down in the bed and prepared to go back to sleep.

Bianca returned to the kitchen where she stood by the
sink, staring blindly into the courtyard. She felt as if she
had been punched in the stomach. That Joe Crawford who,
all this time had been lurking at the back of her mind as a

kind of latter-day Beau Geste, should have been the man who had sent Lucy flying into the house in tears was a blow which made her mind reel.

Peter would not be surprised. He had warned her that Joe was the type whose urges could get out of hand. She had thought at the time that his judgment was clouded by jealousy, but perhaps it had not been. Perhaps *her* judgment had been clouded by Joe's strong appeal to her senses.

Presently her sick sense of disillusionment became charged with anger. Very rarely did Bianca lose her temper, and then usually in defence of someone else—but when her wrath was aroused, it burned with a white-hot flame not easily douched.

Half an hour later, mounted on Lucy's red moped, she was on her way into town, no longer with the object of going to the market, but resolved to seek out Joe Crawford and tell him exactly what she thought of him.

CHAPTER THREE

IN her agitated state of mind, Bianca forgot that Peter had mentioned that Joe Crawford's boat was berthed next to *Sheila*. Not knowing the name of Joe's boat, when she arrived at the harbour she spoke to a woman who was hanging out washing on a Dutch boat.

'Excuse me, do you know where I can find Joe Crawford?'

'Oh, yes. Joe's boat is the one at the end of the quay. Her name is *La Libertad*.' The woman sounded as if she knew him, and liked him.

'Thank you.'

'You're welcome.'

Bianca remounted the moped and rode slowly past a motley assortment of vessels, their ports of registry ranging from Hamburg to Guernsey and Long Island.

La Libertad—*Freedom*—was not moored close to the quay's edge like many of the others, but was separated from it by several yards of water. The double doors leading to the area between decks were open, but there was no sign of her owner.

Bianca parked her moped and, cupping her hands round her mouth called, 'Mr Crawford? Are you there, Mr Crawford?'

At first the only response to her shout was an outburst of barking, followed by the appearance of a short-coated, bushy-tailed mongrel which rushed round from somewhere on the foredeck and barked at her from the cockpit.

As its tail was wagging, she concluded it was not unfriendly but was merely fulfilling its duties as watchdog.

A few moments later Joe appeared, clad in a faded pair of denim shorts, and looking even more bronzed than the last time she had seen him.

'Ah, Bianca,' he said.

For the first time it struck her that when he had brought Lucy home last night he must have recognised the house. No doubt that was why he had driven away from it so speedily.

'I'd like to speak to you,' she said.

Barefoot, his long legs as brown as his torso, he swung himself over the side and down the ladder to the boat's rubber dinghy. This, propelling himself by means of the mooring lines of his own boat and neighbouring vessels, he brought alongside the steps near where she was standing.

Looking up, he said, 'Come aboard.'

'If you don't mind, I'd rather talk here.'

'As you wish.' He made fast the dinghy and came up the steps to her level. 'I gather this isn't a social visit.'

'Hardly,' she said, in a clipped voice.

'What can I do for you?'

'Were you drunk last night?' she asked stiffly. 'Or are you so completely unprincipled that what you did to my stepsister doesn't bother you?'

'Oh, she's your stepsister, is she? What did she tell you I did to her?'

'She said very little,' said Bianca. 'She was too terrified and distraught. I only want to make it clear that if you bother her again, we shall make a complaint to the Guardia. In fact'—she went on, rather recklessly—'if it weren't for not wanting Lucy to have to describe how you treated her, my stepfather would have gone to the Guardia today, and it's more than likely they'd order you to leave the country.

They're not lenient with troublemakers, especially foreign ones.'

'No, you're right, they aren't,' he agreed equably. 'Which is why your stepfather should think twice before making rash accusations. He *is* an *extranjero*, I'm not. As I've spent some years serving this country as a *legionario*, I think they're rather more likely to take my word than that of a flighty little English piece who hangs about bars and discos, and behaves in a way which no responsible Spanish parents would allow with a girl of her age.'

Bianca flushed, unable to deny that Lucy's behaviour might well give a bad impression. Before she could retort that even if her stepsister's conduct was misleading, it didn't excuse his maltreatment of her, Joe went on, 'You say she said very little. She must have said something, presumably? Of what, precisely, am I accused?'

'She told me that on the way home you drove the car off the road and . . . and behaved like the worst kind of brute.'

'Is that so?' he said, still calmly. 'And what did she do? Did she defend her virtue? Or was she too frightened even to struggle?'

'I—I don't know. It seems that, eventually, you came to your senses.'

'I see. And, having met me, you believed her account of the incident? It seemed to you more than likely that I would force myself on a girl of that age?'

Confronting him, suddenly it seemed the most unlikely thing in the world that this tall, brown-skinned man whose whole appearance suggested self-discipline should abuse an immature girl, or even be attracted by one. Now it seemed to Bianca far more likely that he himself had to sidestep feminine overtures from unsatisfied wives and lonely women without a man in their lives.

Aloud, she said, 'Meeting someone twice isn't knowing

them. You might have had too much to drink.' But even as she said this, it was obvious that he had not. Nine months in a house with Ben Hollis had made her all too familiar with the signs of over-indulgence, and Joe had not the look of a man with a hangover. 'Why should Lucy lie?' she demanded.

'Probably in revenge for being given a set-down. Hell hath no fury like a woman scorned, they say, and your little stepsister has been flaunting her charms at me for some time. Last night, by way of a change, she got herself picked up by a very nasty piece of work who must have laced her Cokes with gin, judging by her condition when I intervened and brought her home. It's true that on the way back I did stop the car for a short time, but not off the road, and if I was brutal to her, it wasn't as she's alleged. The fact is I couldn't drive with her being, as she seemed to think, seductive, so I gave her a short, sharp lecture. After that, apart from a flare-up when I dropped her off, she spent the rest of the way sulking. Maybe I should have handed her over to you, but the car was a borrowed one, and I'm not employed at El Delfin to play nanny to silly little girls.'

He paused and, after a moment, added, 'You can believe me or not, as you like, but there are a good many witnesses to what was happening before I took charge of her, and no one else felt much concern for her welfare. They all seemed to take it for granted that if she went off with the guy who was making her tight, it wouldn't be a new experience for her.'

Bianca was silent. She accepted that what he had told her was the truth, and was ashamed that she had jumped to such a base conclusion about him on no better evidence than the word of a girl who, although not an habitual liar, had many other weaknesses of character.

Before she could find the words to apologise for her mistake, Joe drawled, 'So you took me for a chaser of nymphets, did you? You were way off beam. Although my girlfriends are usually about half the age of the men you seem to prefer, they're several years older and wiser than little sister Lucy. Girls like yourself, who know the score.'

Before Bianca could refute this implication, and regardless of who might be watching, he crossed the short distance between them and took her firmly in his arms.

It was not a long kiss and yet, in the space of a few seconds, he managed to make her feel as, before, she had felt only after much kissing with Michael. Joe's lips were warm and tasted faintly of toothpaste, and his skin smelt of some light after-shave, not the heavy *colonias* used by most Spanish men. Briefly, she felt herself pressed against the hard wall of his body, his left arm enclosing both her arms, and his other hand cupping her head so that she could not turn her face to avoid the pressure of his mouth.

Not that her reactions were swift enough to have resisted so sudden and unexpected an attack—if a kiss could be called an attack. But that was precisely what it felt like: a raid not only on all her outer defences but also a storming of that private part of herself, the inner Bianca—wild, primitive, earthy—whom even Michael had never reached, or not to the extent of making her dominate the civilised Bianca.

Joe could. She knew in a flash that there was something about Joe Crawford which could make her lose all control of the uninhibited creature who lurked at the heart of her; perhaps at the heart of all women, except that some of them never knew it because they never met a man who could break through the outer, protective shell.

'How dare you!' she exclaimed, when he released her.

It was the civilised woman speaking, not the uninhibited

Bianca who had not minded—had enjoyed!—having his kiss forced upon her.

'In a more private place, I'd dare a lot more than that.' The golden eyes smiled into hers. 'Don't tell me you didn't enjoy it more than being kissed by your middle-aged boy-friend. He's years too old for you, you know. Riding around in that Mercedes isn't going to compensate for the age-gap between you. You need a much younger man to keep you in order.'

'Peter Lincoln is *not* my boy-friend! He and his wife were friends of my mother's. Sheila Lincoln was killed in a road accident—Peter adored her. The only reason he proposed to me that day was because he's desperately lonely, living alone in that big house, and because he knows I'm unhappy.'

'You think so? My guess is that he proposed to you because, when he saw you in my arms, he realised he lusted for you. But it is only lust, believe me. Disregard all that high-minded nonsense about how much you have in common. Unless they're father and daughter, a man of his age and a girl of yours have nothing in common. He wants a comely young bed-mate. You want the luxuries of life.'

'Do I really?' she exclaimed indignantly. 'It so happens that I've refused Peter. Any luxuries I happen to fancy, I'm quite capable of earning for myself. As for accusing him of lust, you shouldn't judge other men by your own standards, Mr Crawford. You may see women as bed-mates, but some prefer a fuller relationship with us.'

'Oh, sure,' he agreed negligently. 'I should myself. But even the fuller relationships are based on sexual attraction. Right now I'd like to have you in my bunk and, although you might not admit it, I think you'd like to be there. Whether we might subsequently find each other equally satisfying in other ways is an open question. Why don't we start to test the point? Come aboard and have coffee with me? Or, if you're nervous of being private with me, we could go for a swim together, and have coffee afterwards at the beach bar?'

She said, untruthfully, 'I'm not in the least nervous of you, but I didn't come to spend all morning here.'

His eyes narrowed slightly. 'No, you came to accuse me of assault, and got mildly assaulted yourself. But I never knew a woman who minded a little brute force, and'—his gaze sweeping over her figure, today clad in a cotton sundress which under his appraising stare suddenly seemed much more décolleté than it was—'you're not the Dresden china type. You wouldn't crush easily.'

Bianca moved towards the moped. 'I must go to the market.'

He followed her. 'If you're busy this morning, how about tomorrow?'

'I shan't have the moped tomorrow. Lucy uses it to go to work.' She saw no reason to mention her bicycle.

'Then I'll come and fetch you. I kept away while I thought you were tied up with Lincoln, but if you aren't involved with him ...' He left the remark unfinished, except for a glint in his eyes which said as clearly as words that, if the field was clear, he meant to continue the offensive which had already laid waste to her outer defences.

She said, 'I don't think I should. To be frank, I'm not in the market for the casual affair which must, I should think, be your object. My life isn't easy as things are. I don't want to add to my problems.'

'My dear girl, you aren't trying to tell me that you only ever go about with a man who declares from the outset that his intentions are honourable?' said Joe, with one dark eyebrow lifted.

'No, of course not—don't be absurd. But I don't usually

go out with men who make it as clear as you have that their only objective is bed.'

'Perhaps it won't be, after tomorrow. I know I want to make love to you. If you give me the chance to find out, I may discover I also want to talk to you.'

Bianca had never met anyone like him: and, to give him his due, she knew that the thoughts he expressed were what most men felt but refrained from saying. It wasn't his bluntness which bothered her, but rather her own vulnerability.

'I'm afraid I'm not free tomorrow,' she said, as she mounted the moped. 'Perhaps some other time.'

'Definitely some other time.' He stepped out of her way. '*Adiós.*'

' '*Diós.*' She rode away, half regretting her refusal to meet him the following day, half relieved to break free from the magnetic field of his virility.

Even after she had done her marketing, all the way home she could still feel the imprint of his audacious kiss.

On arriving home she found Lucy lying on a beach-bed on the terrace, sunning herself in a minimal scarlet bikini.

Evidently she had recovered from her earlier malaise as she greeted Bianca with a casual, 'Hi! Is there anything to eat? I'm starving!'

'Then why not make yourself a snack? There's bread and *chorizo* and cheese in the kitchen. Have you made your bed yet?'

'No, not yet. Does it matter?'

'Not as long as you realise that I'm not going to make it for you.'

Often Bianca had made her stepsister's bed because Lucy seldom rose early enough to do all the things she should do before going to work, and her unmade bed and chaotic room fretted Bianca's sense of order. She was not obsessively tidy, and disliked sitting-rooms which were too neat with no books lying about, or other evidence of their occupants' interests. But spotless bathrooms, made beds and drawers in reasonable order seemed to her basic to comfort.

'You seem in a huff about something,' commented Lucy, following her to the kitchen.

Bianca began to unpack her shopping. 'I'm in more than a huff, Lucy. I'm furious with you,' she said quietly. 'Don't you realise how very wrong it is to make up the sort of defamatory nonsense you told me about Joe Crawford? How could you do such a thing? You should be thanking your stars he was decent enough to bring you home before you made even more of a fool of yourself. To make out to me that *he* was the villain of the piece was a really wicked thing to do.'

'You don't mean you went and told him?' Lucy exclaimed, looking both alarmed and angry.

'Naturally I did. You didn't suppose I shouldn't do anything? In the absence of anyone better, I feel responsible for you.'

'Don't bother: I can look after myself,' the younger girl said resentfully.

'But last night proves that you can't. Joe said you'd been picked up by a thoroughly nasty piece of work.'

'Some people say Joe Crawford isn't a saint,' Lucy retorted. 'He's been in the Spanish Foreign Legion, which is full of all kinds of shady characters, and he didn't buy that big boat with the money he makes from piano-playing. They say the only way he could have afforded it is by getting rich quick from smuggling, probably drugs.'

'I should think that rumour has as much foundation as the story you made up last night,' said Bianca crisply. 'At a guess, I should think the boat belonged to his grandparents who are past the age for strenuous sailing.'

'How do you know he has grandparents? You seem to have got very chummy with him. Don't tell me you fancy him?'

'Peter knows him, and he mentioned them. My conversation with Mr Crawford was about what happened last night. If I were you, I should keep out of his way in future. He wasn't pleased to hear your version of what happened, and he's likely to give you a pretty severe dressing-down the next time he sees you.'

'Oh, Joe Crawford,' said Lucy, causing Bianca to give her a look of mingled exasperation and pity.

Tiresome as her stepsister was, she could not help feeling sorry for a girl so at odds with the world that she went out of her way to alienate the few people who wanted to help her.

An instant later she was surprised to see Lucy flushing and looking embarrassed. Following her sister's glance, Bianca turned and discovered that a young man was standing on the threshold of the open back door.

'Hi,' he said to her, smiling. 'I'm Mark Lincoln. I've just arrived from England, but my father's house is locked up. I believe you people are friends of his. Maybe you know where he is.'

Bianca shook her head. She had not seen Peter for several days. 'No, but I should think he may have gone to Alicante or Valencia for the day. He wouldn't have gone further afield without mentioning it to us. How did you get here?'

'Some friends dropped me off on their way south.'

'You're welcome to wait for your father here. You look rather hot. Would you like a cold beer, and perhaps a shower?'

'That would be marvellous. Thanks.' He came into the

room and dumped down the grip he was carrying.

'I'm Bianca, and this is Lucy. Get Mark a beer, would you, Lucy?'

'Yes, I know your names from my father's letters. I suppose you know about me—that I'm rather a thorn in his side, I mean? Or have been, up to now.'

He sat down on the stool she had indicated. Bianca knew he was nineteen, nearly twenty. The last time Peter had seen him, he had had long hair and a beard, and affected a style of dress which had maddened his conventional father. Now his hair was no longer than Peter's, the beard had gone and his cotton-knit shirt, jeans and track shoes were almost a summer uniform among the young in Spain, whatever their nationality.

She said, 'I know he's worried about you at times, but I never heard him say anything which didn't suggest that he's extremely fond of you.'

By now Lucy had uncapped a bottle of beer for him. She said, 'I'm going to make myself a snack. Can I do one for you?'

'Yes, thank you. I am a bit peckish. We made an early start this morning. In fact, taking turns with the driving, we never really stopped, except to wash and have coffee at the motorway service stations.'

He continued to chat to her while she cut and buttered bread rolls, and filled them with lettuce from a bag of washed leaves in the fridge, and pieces of pâté.

Bianca had bought the pâté for their supper, but she didn't protest as Lucy used most of it up.

Presently she said to the two younger people, 'I'm going to start using the blender, so why don't you two finish your snacks on the terrace? Lucy, will you find Mark a towel when he goes for a shower?'

'Yes, of course,' said her stepsister, in a much more

amiable manner than before his arrival.

Left to herself Bianca went on preparing a large pan of *gazpacho,* a Spanish soup which, served cold, made a refreshing starter for a hot-weather supper, and was full of vitamins. The more Ben drank, the less he ate, but at least she could ensure that Lucy had a balanced diet, which would probably not be the case if Bianca left them. She had learnt to cook by watching her mother, a woman who, although a great part of her life was filled by her profession, had delighted in all the domestic arts. It was therefore no chore to Bianca to cook proper meals rather than dishing up stodgy convenience foods, although she did find it disheartening when, however tasty the meal which she set before him, her stepfather merely picked at it.

As she jointed a yellow-skinned Spanish chicken, her thoughts returned to the man in whose strong arms, a short time ago, she had felt like a swimmer caught by a powerful undertow.

Her instinct warned her that the advice she had given Lucy—to keep out of Joe Crawford's way—was equally applicable to herself. Yet she felt that she owed him not only a proper apology for misjudging him, but also her thanks for his chivalrous intervention. She decided that the best way to make amends and express her gratitude was to cook him a basket of home-made goodies and deliver them, with a note, to El Delfin. That way she could discharge her obligations without further personal contact.

If he then chose to contact her again ... she would cross that bridge when she came to it—if she came to it. Probably he wouldn't bother. That he had kissed her, and declared himself attracted to her, didn't necessarily mean anything. More than likely it was his reaction to any passable-looking female.

*

Bianca's surmise had been correct, and when, late that afternoon, Peter returned from a visit to Alicante, he found his son and the two girls sitting by his swimming-pool. Later he suggested taking them all out to dinner, but Bianca objected on the grounds that as Lucy had been off colour that morning and had not gone to work, it would not do for her to be seen enjoying herself in public.

Knowing that Peter had reservations about eating under Ben's roof—actually the Casa Mimosa belonged to her now—and as Juanita had the day off, she suggested cooking a meal for them at Bellavista. As long as Mark and Lucy were present, Peter was not likely to overstep the limits of friendship, if indeed he ever would again.

The makings of the meal being already prepared, she had only to enlist Mark's help in carrying various containers from one house to the other so that she could re-heat the main course in Peter's split level oven, and cook the vegetables on the gleaming stainless steel hob which was set in the top of an elaborate island unit in the centre of the lavishly fitted kitchen. Although it might have been the envy of many women, Bianca found Peter's kitchen more like an operating theatre than the cosy heart of a home.

They ate outside, by the swimming pool which at night was lit by a revolving rainbow of lights which, combined with three jets of water fountaining towards the centre, made a pretty if somewhat theatrical centrepiece to the garden with its concealed floodlights throwing the foliage of trees and shrubs into dramatic relief.

The Lincolns had spent a great deal of money on their garden, importing palm trees from Elche, a palm-growing centre some way south of Alicante, and buying weathered antique urns and Ali Baba pots as containers for such beautiful plants as the pale yellow, night-scented cestrum, and the red-veined bright orange bell-flowers of the canarina.

Yet although it was small by comparison, in its way the garden laid out by her mother, and planted mostly with cuttings from other gardens, was no less charming than Peter's elaborate grounds.

After dinner, while Mark and Lucy were dancing at the far end of the long veranda which surrounded two sides of the pool, giving shade in the broiling heat of summer, Peter said to her, 'I'm surprised—pleasantly so—by the change in Mark since I last saw him. He's become quite civilised at last.'

'If he were here long enough, he might reform Lucy,' said Bianca. For a change her stepsister was looking happy instead of sulky. 'How long is he staying?'

'A couple of weeks, so he says. He's been offered a partnership in a business, and he came out to ask if I would be willing to back him to the tune of ten thousand pounds. At one time I should have refused point-blank. But it seems that for the past year he's been supporting himself and saving the allowance I've been making him.'

'What kind of business is it?'

'Hand-made furniture for which, apparently, there is a considerable demand. The only thing Mark liked at school was woodwork, but it never occurred to me that it might be the basis of a career.'

'I think people who work with their hands, making one-off objects as opposed to mass-produced things, are usually much more contented than people in so-called executive jobs,' said Bianca thoughtfully.

From Mark their talk turned to gardening and, although it was a subject which usually interested her, tonight she felt a sudden longing to cast off the mantle of sedateness which seemed to have fallen upon her, and to join in the dancing. But not with Peter as a partner. He danced in the style of his youth, when she was a baby, and lacking a natural sense of rhythm was not good at modern dancing.

That night, in her room, instead of reading as she usually did, she spent a long time with a writing pad on her lap, composing a note to Joe. But it wasn't an easy thing to write and after scribbling several beginnings, none of which satisfied her, she sat absentmindedly covering the paper with doodles while remembering all that he had said to her, and she to him, on the quayside that morning.

Did he really prefer girls who, in his phrase, 'knew the score'? Or had that remark been thrown in to annoy her? If he had meant it, it disqualified her from joining the ranks of his girl-friends because, compared with many of her contemporaries, she knew herself to be an innocent. Not that one could always believe appearances. Sometimes they could be misleading. She had once shared a flat with two girls, both of whom had seemed equally worldly until one of them, Jane, had confided that she had never been to bed with a man, and only pretended she had in order to be in the swim.

What am I doing—thinking about being his girl-friend? Bianca asked herself, putting an end to this dangerous train of ideas. With her note to him still unwritten, she put aside the pad and forced herself to concentrate on her bedside book until she was drowsy enough to put out the light without any risk of lying awake, indulging in thoughts which were better unthought.

CHAPTER FOUR

A WEEK later she was in the garden, watering, when a car drew up outside and, with a sudden dryness in her throat, she saw Joe climbing out of the driving seat.

'Good morning. I've come to thank you for the excellent samples of your culinary skills,' he said, as he entered the garden. 'That thick-cut marmalade has been a great improvement to my breakfasts, and the fruit cake took me back to my schooldays and the mercy parcels from Harrods which my grandmother organised sometimes when she thought the stuff we were fed might be getting me down. You're not a professional cook, are you?'

'Oh, no, just a keen amateur. Since I've been living in Spain, it's been something to do. I'm glad you enjoyed the cake, but you needn't have bothered to come all this way out to thank me. Those things were a thank-you to you.'

'I didn't come only to thank you, but to take you sailing. You told me up there'—with a nod at the mountainside where they had met for the second time—'that you'd never been on a sailing boat. Now's your opportunity. We can make a day of it: sail down the coast to a bay where the swimming is good, lunch at the beach bar, and come back to harbour in time for me to run you home before I start work at eight.'

'Oh, I should have liked to, but I can't. Not today, I'm afraid.'

Joe tilted an eyebrow. 'You needn't be nervous. I wasn't planning to show you my etchings.'

'It isn't that. You see, once a week I visit an old lady

53

who lives near here. I could put it off, except that today is her birthday. I can't disappoint her.' She was about to add, 'Perhaps some other time' but bit back the words, knowing she ought not to encourage him.

But he wasn't the type to need encouragement. He said firmly, 'No, I see you can't do that. Pity. Never mind, we'll postpone the sailing and just go swimming for an hour. Off you go to fetch your bikini. I'll finish this for you'—taking the watering-can from her.

At the thought of the sea, blue and sparkling, Bianca weakened. In her bedroom she committed what she knew to be another act of weakness by putting on her best bikini and, over it, a beach wrap of turquoise towelling. After stuffing a towel, some sun cream, and a zip-case containing a comb, lipstick and tissues into a straw basket of the kind carried by Spanish country people on their way to tend their vines and almonds, she locked up the house and scribbled a message to Ben.

He had gone to the village for cigarettes, and would probably stop at the bar and stay there till lunch-time. If he did return earlier, there was another key hidden in the garden. He wouldn't be locked out.

It was not until Joe opened the gate for her, and she stepped into the roadway, that she saw the car he had come in was one of a fleet owned by a local firm.

'You didn't rent this specially, did you?' she asked, in dismay.

'Why not? I often rent a car if I want to nip down to Alicante or go walking on Bernia,' he answered, referring to one of the mountains in the region.

'But hiring a car is so expensive, and just to take me swimming ...' she protested.

He opened the passenger's door for her. 'In you get, and stop worrying. You're not committing yourself to anything you wouldn't like. I very rarely make passes at girls before lunch. The other day was an exception. Being angry makes you very kissable. Today, if you keep your cool, you'll be perfectly safe with me.'

Watching him walk round the bonnet after he had closed the door on her, she saw laughter pulling at the corners of his mouth.

The car was a small one, made to seem smaller by Joe's length of leg and breadth of shoulder. After driving a short way, he asked, 'How has young Lucy been behaving since she and I tangled? I haven't seen her around lately.'

'No, I think she's nervous of what you might say to her. Also Peter Lincoln's son is out here for a short time. He's not quite twenty, a nice boy. They seem to get on rather well.'

'So that's one weight off your mind, at least for the time being. But there are others, I gather?'

'Only one other—my stepfather. He has a drinking problem, which is why I can't go back to England and leave Lucy with him. Not that I particularly want to. I love Spain. I'm very happy here, or could be, in different circumstances. But I can't earn my living here, or not as I used to in England.'

'What did you do there?'

'Genealogical research. I can't do it here, and even my basic skills like typing and speed-writing aren't much use without better Spanish. As I've been here nine months you might think I should be quite fluent, but in fact for most of that time I was nursing my mother. She died about three months ago, and since then I've been trying to improve. But as most of the people round here speak Valenciano, I don't really get enough practice.'

'No, that's always a problem. To acquire real fluency in a language you have to live with the people who speak it, with little or no opportunity to fall back on your own language.'

'As you did when you joined the Spanish Legion?'

'Yes. There was a German recruit in my intake who spoke some English, but after our basic training we weren't in the same *compania*, so for nearly a year I spoke nothing but Spanish.'

'What made you join?' she asked. 'Peter said you went in at eighteen, which seems very young to enlist in a thing like the Legion. Did you never have cold feet?'

'Oh, yes—very cold,' he said dryly. 'I signed on in Madrid, and then we were taken by lorry to Valencia and, from there, shipped to Fuerteventura in the Canaries. I remember that during that voyage two years seemed like forever. But once we arrived and started training it wasn't so bad. I enjoyed it.'

He had still not explained his enlistment, and somehow she did not like to press for the reason. Glancing sideways, she tried to imagine him as an eighteen-year old; full-grown physically, no doubt, but still with a good deal of boyishness about him. Not the man he was now; strong, self-reliant, too much in command of himself ever to become like Ben, and equally in command of difficult situations such as when he had rescued Lucy from a man who might have cut up rough.

This is madness. I'm making a superman of him, and what do I really know of him? Bianca thought vexedly. He must have his faults, like all men. Perhaps his attitude to women was one of the flaws in his character. He might be an incurable womaniser. Not only that, but incapable of ever settling anywhere so that any woman he married would have to live like a gypsy, never settled, never secure.

Except that a man like Joe is, himself, the best kind of security, one part of her mind argued against the other part. Who wants a mortgage and life insurance? Life is for living, and with him I should really live.

The direction of her thoughts appalled her. And yet, deep down, she had known from the first time she saw him that here was a man who was capable of making her life as chaotic as Lucy sometimes left her room. But a room could be put back in order, and Bianca had reason to know that emotions, once thrown into chaos, were not as easily restored to their former good order.

He took her to a small beach in the shelter of steep reddish cliffs where a rocky beach shelved into the water pale aquamarine at the edge, quickly shading to deep blue-green further out.

When Bianca unbuttoned her beach robe she knew Joe was watching her, and was glad of the flattering cut of the brown and black French bikini, an extravagant twentieth birthday present from her mother. Made of silk, and silk-lined, in spite of its brevity it did things for her figure not done by her chain store bikinis.

Together they waded into the sea, until Joe plunged under the surface and she followed him. She came up long before he did, and trod water, looking around until he emerged, yards away, and struck out with a powerful crawl which, had they surfaced together, she could not have matched for more than a stroke or two. She swam well, but not like he did.

Some time later, while she was floating, her face turned up to the sun, her mind blank with contentment, she felt a disturbance in the water beneath her and righted herself to find him coming up near her.

'Are you ready for coffee, or vino?'

She nodded. Together they swam for the shore, his leisurely back stroke making it possible for her to keep alongside him until, in the shallows, they stood up. He reached for her hand to help her to cross a stretch of stones.

He had excellent manners, she had noticed, and his reference to mercy parcels from Harrods suggested an expensive schooling. What was his background? And why was a man of his age and apparent education not engaged in one of the professions, but scratching a living as a player of what she had once heard called 'wallpaper music'?

They both towelled their heads, leaving the drops of salt water which glistened on their skin to evaporate in the heat. Bianca combed her short hair back into shape. In fifteen minutes it would be dry. Then they went up the steps to the beach bar where, on the awning-shaded terrace, one table had just become vacant.

Joe ordered a beer for himself and a glass of *rosado* for her.

'Shall we have *calamares*?' he suggested.

'Yes, if you'll let me go Dutch.'

'I may not run a Mercedes, but I'm not yet so broke I can't afford to buy a few *tapas*,' he said, rather sardonically.

She had not meant to offend him. She had to be careful herself, and assumed that his funds were stretched too. But perhaps she was wrong.

Presently, when the waiter had brought their drinks, he said, 'Tell me more about this genealogical research you used to do in England. Did you work at the College of Arms?'

'No, the College is mainly concerned with titles—helping life peers to choose their new ones, or advising people who think they have a claim to or some connection with an old one. Most of the clients of the man for whom I worked weren't interested in their forebears for snobbish reasons; they wanted to know where their roots were. I think as modern society becomes increasingly mobile, and more and more people have to live in cities and apartments, they feel a hunger for the old ways; the quiet, settled lives of their ancestors, and the greater sense of community.'

'How do you go about tracing their pasts for these people?' Joe asked her.

'Sometimes it's simple, sometimes it can be very complicated.'

She began to explain how it was done; the excitement of following the clues which led further and further into the past, sometimes losing the way or arriving at an apparent dead-end, but then finding another way round the seemingly impassable obstacle.

It was the first time, in Spain, that anyone had expressed an interest in her work. Presently, with the arrival of their dish of *calamares*, she realised that she had been talking for some time, and might have been boring him.

'Not at all,' he said, when she apologised. 'No specialist speaking on his or her subject is ever boring. And had I been bored—which I wasn't—I had you to look at.'

Bianca was sitting well back from the table to keep her legs in the sun, and his hazel eyes travelled slowly from her slim bare shoulders to her knees, taking in all the lightly concealed curves in between.

Bianca leaned forward to take a toothpick from a pot of them on the table, and used it to spear a ring of squid fried in batter and still hot from the pan so that some caution was necessary in biting through the outer crispness to the slightly rubbery white flesh. She was glad they were surrounded by people. If, merely by looking at her like that, Joe could make her skin tingle, what would be the effect if they were alone and he touched her?

He said, 'I must introduce you to old Rufus Fisher. He's nearly eighty, but looks about sixty. He's looking for some-

one to type his memoirs. Would the job interest you? He's
not short of money—he'd pay. If you haven't a typewriter,
you can borrow mine.'

'I brought my typewriter with me. Yes, I'd be very
interested.'

'He isn't on board at the moment, or I'd take you along
straight away.'

'Oh, he lives on one of the boats?'

'Yes, he's spent his whole life at sea. He was born on
a boat, and he means to die on one, he says.'

'I could come down tomorrow, on my bike,' suggested
Bianca. 'I sometimes do, for an early swim.'

'It must be a hot ride home, isn't it?'

'Yes, it is a bit. I shan't do it in August, if I'm still here
then, which I suppose I shall be.'

'Has Lucy no relations in England who would give her
a home for a year or two?'

Bianca shook her head. 'No, no one, and anyway the
last thing she wants is to go to England. She prefers it
here. The idea of a nine-to-five job in a colder climate
doesn't appeal to her at all.'

'If your stepfather hits the bottle I should have thought
Spain, where booze is still fairly cheap, is not a good place
for him to live,' commented Joe.

'No, I know it isn't. But he does scrape a small living
here, when the mood takes him. He can do a painting in
three hours, and sell it for two thousand pesetas, which
even after deducting the cost of materials, and the com-
mission taken by the bar where it was on show, is not
bad for a morning's work.'

'Very good,' he agreed.

'He couldn't do the same in England. So if I were to
force the issue by selling the house over their heads, I'm not
sure it would be an improvement on our present situation.'

'The house belongs to you, does it?'

'Yes, it was my mother's home, not Ben's. He and Lucy lived in a rented place before he and Mother married.'

Even as she confided this information, she felt a faint pang of misgiving. Joe's question could represent nothing but an innocent interest in her dilemma. But when she had first come to Spain, the principal topic of conversation had been the activities of a confidence trickster who had gulled a number of people into parting with large sums of money, and one lonely widow had been on the brink of signing over her property before the police had caught up with him.

Joe could be as honest as she was. But what did she really know about him?

Shortly afterwards he drove her home. At her gate, he said, 'We'll make a date to go sailing when I see you to-morrow.'

Ben had watched her come home from the veranda. As the car drove away and his stepdaughter mounted the steps, he said, 'Found yourself a boy-friend, Bianca?'

She shook her head. 'An acquaintance of Peter's who may be able to put some secretarial work my way. I stretch our funds as far as I possibly can, Ben, but the cost of living is rising and the house is overdue for a coat of paint. You're going to have to produce more pictures, or we shan't make ends meet for much longer.'

'Oh, don't nag, girl,' he told her irritably. 'You must take after your father. Carla never fussed about money the way you do. I'm paying my way and Lucy gives you as much as she can. You're the only one who's not work-ing.'

He gulped down the rest of his drink, and went indoors to pour another.

Bianca sighed. It was a waste of time talking to him. A

non-smoker herself, sometimes she found his nicotined fingers and aura of brandy, not to mention the laden ash-trays which he never emptied, almost more than she could bear. She would have liked to tell him to get out, but she couldn't because of her promise to look after Lucy. Not that Lucy ever showed much affection for her father, but he was her father and perhaps, under an offhand manner, she concealed some of the love which Bianca had felt for her own father.

Joe was on deck when she arrived at his mooring next morning. He did not notice her approaching because he was sitting in the cockpit sewing a button on a shirt. Another shirt and a pair of shorts were drying on a line fixed to the rigging. Bianca thought how agreeable it must be to live with a man who could keep his clothes clean and mended, and was not dependent on a woman always to attend to them for him, as Ben was.

'Good morning,' she called.

He looked up and smiled. 'Hello there. I'll be right with you.'

He tossed the shirt on one side and came ashore, accompanied this time by the mongrel which had barked at her on the occasion of her first call on his master. The dog bounded up the landing steps ahead of him, and Bianca made friendly overtures. He wagged his tail, but avoided her attempt to pat him.

'Fred's a little leery with people he hasn't met before. His experience of human beings hasn't always been good, and although he's been living with me for over a year now, he still reserves judgment until he's met someone a few times,' said Joe, as he came up the steps.

He put out his hand and automatically she responded, thinking he had fallen into the Spanish habit of shaking hands with every greeting and parting, although he had not done it yesterday. But when he continued the hand-clasp for far longer than normal, she knew he was flirting with her.

To withdraw her hand was impossible until he chose to release it. In an effort to appear unconcerned, she said, 'What do you mean?—About his experience of human beings?'

The warm, teasing light in his eyes was suddenly changed to a look which, brief as it was, afterwards she could not forget.

He said, 'I found him in a wood in England—tied up in a sack and left to starve. If he hadn't been too weak by then, no doubt he'd have sunk his teeth into me.'

She forgot, for a moment, her discomfiture. 'Oh, how *could* anyone be so vile!'

'How indeed? But there are people who do things like that to animals which they don't want but are too mean to have put down humanely by a vet or the R.S.P.C.A.' The cold gleam went out of his eyes. 'Anyway Fred survived, and seems to enjoy being a seadog.'

There was a pause.

'You're still holding my hand,' said Bianca.

Joe looked down at her, smiling slightly, the last trace of anger banished. 'Do you dislike it?'

'I—I think it must look rather strange.'

'Not to anyone who saw us last time.'

The reminder of how much more closely they had come into contact before made her cheeks hot with sudden shyness.

'Shouldn't we go and see your friend?'

He laughed, and let go her hand. 'Okay. Come on, Fred!' With a whistle to the dog, which had wandered off, he began to stroll along the quay.

The boat to which he took her had *Pago Pago* written on her stern.

'Pronounced as if spelt Pango Pango,' said Joe, seeing her noting the name. 'It's a port somewhere in the South Seas, and apparently in that part of the world a "g" has an "ing" sound.'

Unlike his own boat, *Pago Pago* was moored close up to the quay. Fred leapt aboard and went below, and shortly afterwards the boat's owner appeared. Had Joe not told her his true age, Bianca would have taken Rufus Fisher for a man who had been able to retire to a life in the sun several years before the usual age. Her first thought, on seeing his bronzed face and still-thick white hair, was that this was probably how, in fifty years' time Joe would look. Mr Fisher's flesh had lost the elasticity of Joe's skin, but he was still a fit, active man whom no casual observer would suspect of having been born at the turn of the century.

When Joe introduced him, he said, 'I'm delighted to meet you, Miss Dawson. Joe has led me to hope that you may be willing to assist me. Come aboard.' He offered a gnarled but strong hand to help her to step across the gap between quay and stern, and to step down into the cock-pit.

When she saw the cleanness and order of his living space, she realised he must be like Joe in his competence to look after himself. Perhaps all sea-going men were. However, his neatness did not extend to the contents of a suitcase which he brought from his sleeping quarters. It was cram-med with an extraordinary assortment of papers which he wanted sorted out and arranged in some way which made easy reference possible.

'Could you do that for me, Miss Dawson?' he asked.

'Certainly.'

'Splendid. When can you start?'

'Now, if you wish.'

'Excellent. I'll leave you to it while I go up to the market. I'll be back about noon. Please feel free to make yourself coffee or to have a drink while I'm gone.' He showed her where things were kept in the tiny galley amidships.

'There are one or two things I need in town. I'll walk up with you,' said Joe. 'See you later, Bianca.'

The two men went ashore, leaving her to tackle the muddle in the suitcase.

About an hour later, by which time she had begun to form some idea of the scope of the collection, and how it might best be arranged, she heard someone coming aboard.

'How are you getting on?' enquired Joe, coming below.

'It's a fascinating record of a life. It goes right back to early school reports.'

Joe glanced at a pile of letters, still in envelopes bearing stamps from all parts of the globe, and addressed to Mrs Hugo Brett.

'Mrs Brett was his sister who kept all this stuff. She was an inveterate hoarder and when she died a short time ago, and Rufus went back to England to wind up her affairs, he found all this in a drawer and thought it might be a useful aid to his memory.'

'Ah, I see. I wondered how he came by it. One doesn't think of boat people being collectors. They haven't room to amass things.'

'No, on boats the less clutter the better. But even for life ashore, possessions tie people down. They become an encumbrance. Half the things people own are quite unnecessary. I'm in favour not only of travelling light, but of living light, too. No excess baggage.'

Would he count a wife as excess baggage? Bianca found herself wondering.

She said, 'One must have some personal things, surely? Or how can one make a place homely?'

'A few things, yes,' he agreed. 'But not a pantechnicon-load of them. Did you make yourself some coffee?'

She shook her head. 'I was too absorbed in all this.'

'I'll make some for us both.'

She expected him, before she went home, to arrange their sailing date, but he made no reference to the subject, whether because he had forgotten or because he had changed his mind she could not be sure.

The next day she went again to spend several hours sorting the accumulation of papers into temporary storage in plastic bags.

On some of the letters written by Rufus to his sister, the postmark was indecipherable. When she mentioned this to him, he said, 'Look inside at the dates on the letters. None of them is private. In fact I'd be much obliged if you'd make it part of your task to read through them, and put on one side those which seem to have something of interest in them.'

Later on, he said, 'I expect you're wondering why an unimportant old josser like m'self should bother to scribble his memoirs. Two reasons. The first is for mental exercise. One sees too many people who, once they've retired, let their brains rust. The other reason is that, never having a wife or children, I'd like to leave something to posterity. My jottings won't be worth publishing now—I know that. But if I deposit them in a record office, it could be that in a hundred or two hundred years' time, they might throw some interesting light on how people lived in my day.'

He gave her a sharp look from under his beetling white eyebrows. 'And if you're wondering why I remained a bachelor, it was not for lack of interest in women. But the only one I wanted to marry was already married, unfortunately. Nowadays, no doubt, we'd have run off together. But it wasn't done then—or not often. What about you, young woman? Are you one of this new breed of females who don't need a man to look after them?'

'I don't actually need one, but I think it must be very nice to have one,' said Bianca, smiling. 'I must admit I'm glad I wasn't born at a time when I should have had to accept a husband urged on me by my parents, or when there were very few ways for me to support myself. But I'm not so advanced that I think of marriage as obsolete.'

'Very sensible views—very sensible,' the old man said, nodding approvingly. 'Mind you——'

From where he was sitting, he could see who was passing along the quay, and he broke off his next remark to hail someone and call them aboard for a mid-morning noggin.

'Come up to the cockpit, Bianca, and have ten minutes in the sun,' he urged her.

She stepped up as Joe stepped down, and her pulses quickened as he smiled and said good morning to her. He was carrying a towel, snorkel and flippers and was evidently on his way to the beach.

Rufus poured out three bottles of chilled lager. 'We've just been talking about marriage. What are your views, Joe?' he enquired.

'If I could find a rich widow who would keep me on a fairly long leash, I'd snap her up at once,' Joe said lightly.

Rufus laughed, and Bianca joined in. But it flashed through her mind that the younger man might not be joking, and the older one, knowing this, might have asked him a leading question in order obliquely to warn her that Joe was a dangerous man for a girl to become too fond of.

He did not stay long, not did he mention taking her sail-

ing. The next day she did not see him, and the day after
that his boat was not at her moorings, so he must have
gone sailing alone or with someone else, she thought, rather
forlornly.

That evening, Mark's last night, Peter took his son and
the two girls to dine at an expensive restaurant.

Bianca wore a dress she had made from a length of silk
crêpe-de-chine, a relic of the 1930s which her mother had
found in a box of old clothes in a junk shop. Carla had
loved beautiful fabrics and refused to wear anything syn-
thetic, dismissing the convenience of man-made materials
as of little account compared with the look and feel of
linen and silk. Bianca had made up the material in a rather
Thirty-ish style with shoe-string straps and godets set in
the skirt so that it swirled when she walked. In England she
would have worn palest green Dior tights to match the
colour of the silk, but in Spain now, even at night, the
sheerest tights were too hot, and her legs were golden-
brown and satiny from daily applications of bath lotion
after her shower. With the dress she wore only a thread-
fine gilt chain round her throat, and tiny mock-diamond
stars in her ears.

'You always look right for every occasion,' said Peter.
appreciatively, when he saw her.

'Thank you.' She had a moment's misgiving in case, in
spite of the presence of Mark and Lucy, he might find a
way, later, to revive the subject she hoped had lapsed for
good.

They started their meal with chilled avocado soup. As
she laid down her spoon after the last creamy mouthful,
and glanced round the restaurant, Bianca was startled to see
the head waiter bowing a welcome to Joe. He was not
alone. Beside him was a woman who, as they moved to a
table for two, drew more eyes than Bianca's to her.

She was some years older than Joe, perhaps even in her late thirties, and she had all the hallmarks of wealth. The enormous solitaire diamond which glittered on her wedding ring finger, the simplicity of her white dress, the elegance of her pale grey lizardskin sandals and small matching bag and, above all, the condition of her hair, skin and nails betokened a woman long used to luxury.

Could it be, Bianca thought, gazing at them, that Joe had found his rich widow?

Not wishing him to catch her staring at them, she quickly averted her gaze. The next time she ventured a look, Joe was hidden from view by a party of people at a table in the centre of the room. But his companion was still visible and, as Bianca was looking at her more closely, she saw they were toasting each other in what was probably real champagne rather than the Spanish sparkling wine which most people drank on special occasions. The next thing she saw was Joe's strong brown hand reaching for the woman's delicate hand, after which Bianca had a quick glimpse of his face as he leaned forward to kiss the backs of his companion's fingers.

That the gesture pleased the woman was obvious. She responded with a smile which made it plain that, if their relationship was not already a close one, it would not be long before it was. And Bianca could see that, from a man's point of view, such a liaison would probably be as enjoyable as and less troublesome than a love affair with a young woman.

'You don't seem to be enjoying the *paella* as much as usual,' commented Peter.

'Oh, yes, I am—of course I am,' she said hastily, beginning to eat it with a greater display of enjoyment.

By now it was clear that Lucy had lost her heart to Mark, and he seemed to feel the same way; but Bianca thought it was probably a holiday romance and unlikely to survive the long interval before they would see each other again. She wished Mark was staying in Spain. Under his influence Lucy had stopped being difficult, and become quite biddable and blithe.

'I shan't be alone for long,' Peter said to her presently. 'I heard from Philip today. He and Janet are coming out for a week. They arrive on Saturday.'

Bianca had not met his elder son and his wife, but she knew a good deal about them.

'Are they bringing the children?' she asked.

'No, they're leaving them with Janet's parents. Philip says Janet needs a rest. She had 'flu during the winter, and it's left her run down. A week in the sun, with nothing to do but relax, will do her a world of good. Which reminds me, before we leave here tonight I'll book a table for the four of us to dine here next week.'

He took it for granted that she was free, as indeed she was, thought Bianca despondently. The only man with whom she would have liked to dine here was otherwise engaged, and very likely couldn't afford to pick up the bill at this kind of restaurant anyway. No doubt the woman in white would discreetly attend to it.

It was strange how, with the right man, a cheap meal could be a feast. When Michael had seemed the right man for her, he had seldom been able to take her to the best restaurants, but she had been perfectly content to have supper in one of the several Pizzalands in the part of London where they both lived. A bubbling hot Pizza Special had been as much as she could eat, and with a carafe of wine and coffee afterwards had cost very little and given her as much pleasure as a meal served by waiters, with soft light and pink damask tablecloths.

'I'm going to the cloakroom. Coming, Bianca?' Lucy

asked, at the end of the meal.

Bianca rose to accompany her. In the cloakroom, Lucy said eagerly, 'You know how you've often tried to persuade me to go to England, and I didn't want to? Well, I've changed my mind. Mark says I'd have far more fun, living in London. He has a friend whose sister has a flat there. He's going to find out if she has room for me.'

This reversal of Lucy's previous attitude was not altogether unexpected and the older girl thought it politic, at this stage, to say, 'Why not? Perhaps he could also ask her about job prospects.'

The restaurant was arranged with an island of tables in the centre surrounded by a fairly narrow service aisle between the central tables and those by the walls and windows. When the two girls had walked to the cloakroom, they had taken the most direct route. But when they returned to the restaurant that way was temporarily blocked by the pudding trolley, and by some people pausing to chat to friends. Rather than edge a way through this bottleneck, Lucy went round the other way, leaving Bianca no choice but to follow her. She could only hope that Joe was too absorbed in his companion to notice her passing their table, and she was careful to keep her eyes on her stepsister's back, and pretend to be unaware of his presence.

However, as she came abreast of where they were sitting, he rose and intercepted her.

'Good evening, Bianca.'

'Oh ... good evening,' she answered, affecting surprise.

'Helen, this is Bianca Dawson. Helen is an admirer of your mother's paintings,' he added.

'And the owner of several,' said the woman, smiling at Bianca. 'I used to buy at least one at each private view. I was very sorry to learn that I shall not be able to continue, unless some of your mother's earlier work comes on the market again.'

Bianca glanced at Joe who was still on his feet. 'I don't remember telling you about my mother.'

'No, someone else did.'

'I see.' Who? she wondered. To Helen—whose surname he had neglected to mention—she said, 'Have you come to live in Spain?'

'No, I'm thinking about buying a holiday house, but I feel the south may suit me better than this area. Somewhere down near Marbella perhaps. This region seems rather quiet. Joe tells me this is really the only first class restaurant.'

'Yes, I believe so. There are some good smaller places ... a fishermen's bar, and a place which caters to lorry drivers and has excellent food but a fairly crude *ambiente*,' replied Bianca.

However good the food might be, she could not picture this woman enjoying a supper served on a bare plastic table with a television at full volume and Spanish workmen and drivers conversing at the tops of their voices. Her mother had done so, but Carla had been capable of enjoying life in all its aspects.

'May I give you my card? Then if you should happen to know of a painting by your mother which is for sale you could let me know.' The woman fished in her bag and produced a small gold card case. She took one from it and handed it to Bianca, saying, 'Or if you are ever in London and would like to see the paintings I have, do telephone me.'

'Thank you. I hope you enjoy your visit. Goodbye.' With a smile which included them both, Bianca walked back to Peter's table.

He and Mark did not rise as she returned, and she

could not help contrasting their manners with Joe's. But perhaps if one's object was to captivate a wealthy widow, punctiliousness was a stock-in-trade. Peter's manners were never offensive, but he could not be described as a suave man. Anyway, she was inclined to think that men who were too suave were often not as nice at heart as the slightly rougher diamonds.

'I shouldn't have thought he could have afforded to eat here,' remarked Peter, as she sat down. Obviously he had watched her interchange with them. 'Perhaps piano players are better paid than one would think. Who is that with him?'

Bianca looked at the card. 'Mrs Anthony Russell. Chelsea Park Gardens, London S.W.3,' she told him. 'She's a collector of Mother's paintings.'

'How did she know who you were?'

'Joe told her. I don't know who told him. I didn't.'

In her absence Peter had ordered more coffee and liqueurs. After they had been served, he said, 'I suppose she picked him up at El Delfin, or he picked her up.'

'Possibly.' It was not a subject which she wanted to prolong. To turn the conversation away from the couple on the far side of the room, she said, 'Mark has succeeded where I failed. He's managed to convince Lucy that she'd have a much more interesting life in England.'

At that moment his son and her stepsister were deep in a conversation of their own. To Bianca's surprise Peter looked at them for a moment, then looked at her, and said, 'In that case, in my opinion, he's done her a disservice. The life she has here is not only healthier, but has far fewer pitfalls for a girl of her age. On her own in London, God knows what might happen to her.' He lowered his voice a tone. 'Now that Mark seems to have his feet on the right road at last, I don't want anything to divert him from it.'

He enlarged on this point more fully when they returned to his house and, as they had on the night of his son's arrival, he and Bianca sat and watched the other two dancing from the far end of the veranda.

'To revert to the subject raised earlier, I'm not at all keen to see Mark and Lucy become permanently involved,' he said earnestly. 'She's not an intelligent girl, nor has she much common sense. Also, not to beat about the bush, she's encumbered with an alcoholic father who can only become more of a nuisance as time goes on.'

'You haven't tried to put Mark off her, have you?'

'No, no, I shan't say anything to him. The better relationship between us is something I don't want to upset, and anyway I'm quite sure that within a week of getting back he'll have forgotten about Lucy.'

'Yes, perhaps,' Bianca agreed.

She went home before Lucy, and Peter insisted on escorting her the short distance between their houses although a full moon lit the way as clearly as daylight.

To her dismay, half way there, he tucked his hand through her arm which was crooked at the elbow because she was holding the shoulder chain with which she had brought up to date a small *petit-point* pochette evening bag which had once belonged to her grandmother.

'There is only one person, Bianca, for whom I should be willing to involve myself in an attempt to put Hollis back on his feet,' he said. 'Frankly, I think it's too late, but if you thought it worthwhile to have him put in a special clinic for some months——'

'He would never consent to it, Peter. Ben doesn't admit he has a problem.' She quickened her pace, desperately hoping to avoid the second declaration to which his remark, she felt sure, had been a preliminary. 'It was a particularly good *paella* tonight, didn't you think? It's extraordinary how much they can vary from restaurant to restaurant. Oh, Peter, no——'

This as, by tightening his clasp, he forced her to come to a standstill and thereupon kissed her. His embrace was not the inescapable vice-hold which Joe's had been, and she could have pushed him away. Had he been anyone else, she would have done so, without caring if she hurt his feelings.

But Peter, whatever Joe might say about his motives, she did not regard as a middle-aged man with a lust for a much younger woman. She felt sure it was companionship as much as sex which he wanted from her.

Having kissed her, he held her close and murmured, 'I realise now I was too unromantic last time—talking about common interests, instead of how lovely you are. Tonight you look even more beautiful than usual—the loveliest woman in the restaurant.'

He sounded, she thought, with mingled amusement and compassion, like a badly-cast actor in an amateur dramatic society production. The words did not ring true, partly because they were not true—she knew she could never be called beautiful—and partly because they were obviously prompted by what he felt she wanted to hear, rather than what he was impelled to say.

She freed herself from his arms. 'Peter dear, I do wish you'd believe me. I like you very much—as a friend—but I can never marry you. We shouldn't suit each other at all.'

'I don't believe that. We've always got on like a house on fire.'

'As friends—only as friends.'

'I know what the real reason is—you're attracted to that damned hunk of beefcake who was at the restaurant tonight. I'm not a complete fool, Bianca. I saw how you tried to walk past—pretending you hadn't noticed him there, making up to the other woman—and how you looked when he stopped you, the impudent bastard. Good God! Don't you realise he's probably in bed with her by now? He's the type for whom women have only two uses—sex, and whatever he can get out of them in the way of a handsome present for services rendered.'

'Jealousy—particularly groundless jealousy—doesn't suit you, Peter,' she said stiffly. 'I've told you that I don't love you, but even if I did; I should think twice about marrying any man who made a fuss if I so much 'as spoke to anyone else. I think we'd better say goodnight.' She began to walk quickly away.

He followed her. 'I wouldn't be jealous, Bianca. Not in the ordinary way. It's just that I hate to see you wasting time on a fellow with nothing but brawn to recommend him.'

'And backbone,' she retorted swiftly.

'I'm not so sure of that now. It may not have been guts which made a legionnaire of him. For all we know, the alternative may have been worse—a gaol sentence in England.'

'He was eighteen, Peter, and by the sound of it fresh out of boarding school.'

'What makes you think that? If he's made out he was at Eton it only confirms my feeling that he's a mountebank.'

'You didn't feel that about him until you got this mad idea that I'm in love with him,' she said.

'Oh, no, I don't think you're in love. I'm sure it's only a physical thing. You know as much about the real man as you know about Clint Eastwood, but he's the same macho type and that's what affects you.'

The disdain in his tone made her angry enough to fling back at him, 'The word is honcho, actually. Macho is out of date.'

This was something she had learned from Lucy and, for all she knew, the latest vogue word might be different. But it served as a riposte to make him remember the great disparity in their ages, which was something he seemed to forget, or chose to ignore.

'I don't give a damn what the word is. In my vocabulary he's a no-good wastrel who ought to be doing something useful, not strumming a piano and making up to susceptible women. If he was at Eton—which I doubt—he was probably thrown out for being involved in the drug scene.'

'He never said he was at Eton, or at any other public school. He merely remarked that my fruit cake reminded him of cakes sent by his grandmother when he was at school, which suggested that it was a boarding school.'

'You've been making cakes for him, have you? And washing his shirts, and darning his socks for him, perhaps?'

'Joe washes his own shirts, and he doesn't wear socks, I'm glad to say.'

Peter's habit of wearing socks with sandals, and a singlet under his shirt during the cooler months, was another of the minor barriers between them both in age and taste.

'I baked him a cake as a return for his help when I sprained my ankle,' Bianca added. She did not want to tell him the other reason as, although it showed Joe in a good light, it did not reflect well on Lucy and could only increase his dislike of her.

'Which is more than you've ever done for me,' he said pettishly.

It was such an absurd thing to say—since he didn't like cakes and had, in Juanita, an excellent cook to make him the things he did like—that Bianca's sense of humour, never far below the surface, almost quenched her earlier annoyance. But she realised that to laugh would only exacerbate his mood of furious jealousy and, as she had told him a moment ago, jealousy was the trait she disliked more than any other. She had no previous direct experience of it, but she had seen its destructive force at work in other people's relationships.

She said appeasingly, 'Don't let's spoil a pleasant evening by having a silly row, Peter. I have problems enough without being on bad terms with you. But if we're to go on being friends, you'll have to accept that we can only ever be friends.'

'I don't accept it. Why should I? I love you, and I'm sure I can make you love me.'

'No one can *make* another person love them. It either happens or it doesn't. Oh, Peter, look at it sensibly. When I'm the age you are now, you'll be seventy—an old man.'

'Some men are more active at seventy than others at forty.'

Bianca began to lose patience again. 'If you don't object to everyone thinking I married you for your money, I'm afraid I do. I should hate to feel people were whispering about me in that way—and they would. You know they would.'

'No more than they will if you're seen taking cakes to Joe What's-his-name!'

'One cake, and I should think the boat people gossip a good deal less than land people—they have more to do. It's late, and I'm tired. Thank you for the meal. Goodnight, Peter.'

She turned away and, to her relief, he did not follow but stood where she left him, and was still there when, from the shadow of the veranda, she looked back to where they had stood in the moonlight, arguing.

As she creamed off her eye make-up, Bianca was not happy about her handling of his second proposal. At the same time she felt that, for a man of his age, he had not shown a great deal of sense by being so importunate.

She was still at her dressing-table when she was surprised by a scratch at the door a moment before Lucy opened it and looked in. 'Can I talk to you?'

'Yes. You're home early.'

'Mr Lincoln made Mark bring me back. He said he wanted to talk to him. He seemed rather huffy about something. Have you had a row with him?'

Inwardly, Bianca groaned. Surely Peter wasn't going to spoil his better understanding with his son by venting his disappointment in a tirade against Lucy?

'Not a row—a difference of opinion. Oh, I may as well be frank with you, Lucy. Peter's terribly lonely on his own in that house. He needs to marry again, and he thinks I'm a suitable candidate. I don't agree.'

'I should think not,' the younger girl said. 'Why, he's almost as old as Dad, isn't he?'

'Older, actually.'

Carla Dawson had been only nineteen when Bianca was born, and her second husband had been a year her junior. It was over-indulgence in alcohol and lack of exercise which made Ben look nearer to fifty than forty whereas Peter, by keeping fit, looked a few years less than his age.

'I shouldn't think he was good-looking, even when he was young,' added Lucy. 'Mark takes after his mother. I wish I could go with him tomorrow. I would, if he'd take me. But he won't—says I'm too young.'

'Good for Mark! He must really like you, and want what's best for you.'

Although she went to the harbour every day, it was nearly a week before Bianca set eyes on Joe again. The next time they met was when she was stepping ashore, and he was passing along the quay, pulling the trolley provided by the harbour authorities for the boat people to use when they refilled their drinking water containers from a tap at the end of the public quay. Because he was returning the empty trolley to its place, she had no choice but to walk along with him.

'When are you coming sailing with me?' he asked her, after a preliminary enquiry about progress on Rufus's memoirs.

She said, 'I thought you were busy showing Mrs Russell the sights?'

He slanted an enigmatic look at her. 'I spent a couple of days chauffeuring her around, yes. But now she's moved down to Andalucia. How about tomorrow, when you've finished your stint with Rufus?'

Bianca hesitated, remembering how, after kissing her, he had said, *Right now I'd like to have you in my bunk and, although you might not admit it, I think you'd like to be there.* Were there strings attached to his invitation and, if she accepted it, would he take it as a tacit consent to love-making? *He's the type for whom women have only two uses—sex and whatever he can get out of them in the way of a handsome present.* Had Peter's indictment been nothing but an outburst of jealousy, or did it take a man to judge a man?

'All right, tomorrow after work. Thank you,' she answered.

'Don't bother about food—I'll organise lunch. Just bring your bikini and some sun oil. Brown as you are, you could still get a little burnt during several hours at sea,' he warned.

Perhaps in more ways than one, she thought, already half regretting her acceptance. Joe's parting remark did nothing to allay her misgivings.

'I should tell your family that you might be late getting back,' he called after her.

The next day she said to Rufus, 'Joe is taking me sailing this afternoon.'

'Ah, you'll enjoy that,' was his answer. 'She's a lovely boat, *La Libertad*, and his seamanship is first class, a pleasure to watch, not like some of the people one sees who have good boats but sail them like haystacks.'

On impulse, Bianca said, 'Why don't you come with us, Rufus?'

'It's kind of you to suggest it, m'dear, but I fancy that Joe would prefer to have you to himself.'

'Oh, no, I don't think so. At least, he might, but I don't particularly want to have him to myself.'

She had told him something of her background, but not all of it, and he asked, 'You've a young man in England, perhaps?'

'No, no ... it isn't that——' She left her reply unfinished, not knowing quite how to explain herself.

But as she had already discovered, Rufus was extremely shrewd. He seemed to sense what lay at the back of her mind.

'I don't think you need be concerned that Joe might overstep the mark, m'dear. He may be a scamp in some ways, but I'm sure he's an honest fellow, and a gentleman where women are concerned.'

'Do you think so?' Bianca said doubtfully.

Rufus might be quick to divine her unspoken thoughts, but had he the same insight into Joe's mind? And was he right in supposing that the code of behaviour towards women which had held good in the days of his own young manhood was still respected by Joe's generation?

'I'm not suggesting that he wouldn't make advances,' said

Rufus, with a humorous twinkle. 'There'd be something wrong with him if he didn't. You're a very charming young woman, as no doubt you've been told on many occasions. But Joe's not the sort of bounder to make a nuisance of himself if you made it clear that you wanted to keep things on a friendly basis.'

'Did you meet his friend Mrs Russell while she was here?'

'I did indeed. Knowing my liking for Oriental dishes, they very kindly invited me to join them for a meal at the East Indies restaurant one evening. A delightful woman, and knowledgeable on a wide range of subjects. I gather that before her husband's untimely death she travelled all over the world with him. You met her, too, did you?'

'Yes, but only briefly.' She could not repress her curiosity. 'Do you know how she and Joe met?'

'Somewhere in Greece, I believe—or rather in the Aegean.'

'Oh, not here?'

'No, no—I think they've known each other for some time. I remember them agreeing that the sea in the eastern Mediterranean is considerably clearer than off this coast. Possibly they met last summer while Joe was sailing among the Greek islands. Theirs is certainly not a recent acquaintance.'

Presently, walking along the quay from one boat to the other, Bianca pondered this remark and decided that she preferred the idea of Joe picking up Mrs Russell—or vice versa—at El Delfin to the possibility of their involvement while her rich and presumably older husband was alive.

Joe had seen her leaving *Pago Pago*, and had brought his rubber dinghy to the foot of the landing steps by the time she arrived at the head of them. He gave her a hand to step inboard, waited until she was sitting on the wooden thwart, and began the manoeuvre she had seen before.

When they came alongside *La Libertad*, he held the dinghy steady while she grasped the short three-runged ladder and climbed into the cockpit where, having barked once or twice and sniffed her bare brown feet, Fred retired to his place on the foredeck.

'I'll just show you where the heads are, and then we'll get going. The full tour can wait until later,' said Joe, when he had secured the dinghy astern.

He led her below, through a day cabin upholstered and curtained in silvery olive-leaf needlecord and matching plain linen, and rapped his knuckles on two adjoining doors. 'Lavatory ... washroom.'

'You're even neater than Rufus,' she remarked, on the way back to the cockpit.

'Have to be neat on a boat. Are you an untidy person?' he asked her, with a cocked eyebrow.

'Oh, no, Lucy thinks I'm too tidy—but not as tidy as this.'

The day cabin was as immaculate, and as impersonal, as that on a charter boat. Whatever might be concealed in the bulkhead lockers behind the three-sided banquette, there was nothing on view to indicate that this was a private vessel, or to give any clue to the nature of her owner.

'Can I do anything useful?' she asked, as they stepped up into the sunlight.

He shook his head. 'You've been working all morning. Relax.'

Having watched the commotion when some of the week-end sailors left or entered harbour, with as many as half a dozen people bustling importantly about and getting in each other's way, Bianca was doubly impressed by the economy of effort with which, single-handed, Joe managed.

They left the harbour under power, changing to sail in

the open water of the bay and heading, at first, in the direction of the island of Ibiza which sometimes, on a clear day, could be glimpsed far away on the north-east horizon.

Bianca's only previous experience of looking down on deep water had been from the deck of a Channel ferry. Gliding briskly along under sail was, she quickly discovered, a novel combination of exhilaration and peacefulness. Except now and again, when Joe changed tack and there was a rattle from one of the winches, the splash of a wave against the hull and the sound of the breeze filling the sails were the only noises.

All the clamour of the now-crowded town, the transistor radios, the gabble of Spanish and foreign voices, the sudden crescendo roar of a passing motorbike, the persistent tooting of horns as local drivers caught sight of friends, or tourists in cars cleared a way through icecream-licking, jaywalking pedestrians; all this racket was now left behind with the packed beaches and the pervasive aroma of tanning oils.

'Time for an *aperitivo*,' said Joe.

Bianca had closed her eyes for a few minutes, the better to savour the pleasure of being utterly at peace only a mile, perhaps less, from tourism in full fling. Now, opening them, she found him standing beside her with a tall glass in each hand.

'What is it?' she asked, accepting the one he offered to her.

'Sangria—but not one of the poisonous grape-and-grain mixtures one is sometimes offered at parties. This has only a little brandy in it.'

She sipped the chilled, fruit-flavoured wine. 'Where are we going?'

Now, since going about, they were heading south, in the general direction of Alicante.

'To a bay which, with any luck, we shall have to ourselves. I can do without other people's radios.'

Was that the only reason he hoped for seclusion? she
wondered, with a sudden tremor.

La Libertad crossed the wake of a speeding powerboat
with a lift and dip of her bows for which Joe was prepared
but Bianca was not. The motion caused her to spill a little
of her sangria, but as she was wearing shorts it splashed
harmlessly on her leg. Before she could reach into her basket for a tissue, he brushed the spilt drops from her thigh
with the palm of his hand.

'Sorry about that. I should have warned you we were
going to rock a bit.'

His touch reactivated the tremor. She said, hoping to
sound perfectly calm, 'I suppose you're a very good sailor
—never seasick however rough it is?'

'I wouldn't say never. Not often. But there's no credit in
it. I've known little old ladies who could stand a Force Ten
a lot better than big brawny seamen. You might be a better
sailor than I am.'

'Is a Force Ten the worst kind of weather?'

'No, it's what's known as a whole gale, when the wind is
gusting at between forty-eight and fifty-five miles an hour.
Force Eleven is a storm. Force Twelve is a hurricane, and
Thirteen to Seventeen indicate even worse conditions.'

'What would this wind today be?'

'About Force Three—a gentle breeze. Hold this for me,
would you, for a minute?'

He gave her his glass and went, with surprisingly light
steps for so tall a man, along the narrow footway between
the cockpit and the foredeck to make some adjustment.
When he came back it seemed to her that he sat down a
little closer than he had before. She wondered if she ought
to edge slightly away. But if the change in his position was

unintentional, any movement on her part might make him come closer deliberately. She knew she had never been so aware—not even with Michael—of any man's physical presence. It was like being a pin at the fringe of the field of a magnet. She felt certain that before they returned to harbour Joe would have kissed her again. What she did not know was how she would, or should, react.

In the bay which was their destination, he dropped anchor near a place where the rocks on the sea bed gave place to an area of sandy bottom, and the water was pale blue-green instead of the darker blue of the sea over the rocky parts. From the thickets clinging to the red rock cliffs, which made the beach at their foot inaccessible except by sea, came the concerted chirping of hundreds of cicadas.

'I'll show you where you can change,' he said, when the boat was secure.

'I don't need to change. I'm already in my bikini.' Bianca took off her sun-top and shorts. 'It's hard to judge how deep it is. Deep enough to dive in, presumably?'

'Oh, yes, we're in six metres here. You can dive as deep as you like.'

Half an hour later, sitting under the shade of an awning which Joe had rigged up on the beach, clasping a large *bocadillo* of the kind which Spanish children ate on the way home from school, except that in this case the crusty bread was not filled with cheese or a slab of chocolate but with a shrimp salad mixture, Bianca said, 'Mm ... this is bliss!'

He opened a large cool box he had brought ashore in the dinghy, and produced a bottle of Conde de Caralt *espumoso*, the sparkling wine made by the same method as champagne but, following a French legal action, no longer allowed to be labelled Spanish champagne.

She watched with secret approval as he freed the cork

with a whisper instead of the noisy pop and wasteful over-
flow of foam of the crass show-off. It would have been
better, she thought, if she could have found more to dislike
in him, but almost everything he did only served to en-
hance her approval. He handed her a glass of the pale
golden wine.

'Thank you.' Watching the tiny bubbles rising to the
surface and breaking into a delicate mist, she was reminded
of the night at the restaurant when she had seen him and
Mrs Russell toasting each other.

'What shall we drink to?' he asked.

'My father's favourite toast was "Carpe diem". Did you
take Latin at school?'

He shook his head. 'It had stopped being compulsory by
my time, and anyway I was always among the duds academ-
ically.'

'I imagine you shone on the games field.'

'No, not there either. Team games never appealed to
me, either as a player or an onlooker. I liked sailing and
canoeing at adventure training camps in the holidays, but
neither of those is regarded as a useful qualification for
life.'

'More useful than cricket and football, I should have
thought.'

'On the contrary, rugger and cricket inculcate the all-
important team spirit, in which I was notably lacking,' said
Joe, with a tinge of sarcasm. Bianca received the impression that his schooldays were not a time he remembered
with pleasure. 'Translate "Carpe diem" for me.'

'It means "Seize today" and goes on "and put as little
trust as you can in the morrow".'

'Right: we'll drink to that. Seize today!' he said, lifting
his glass to her.

'Seize today,' she echoed.

'Mm, a glass of cold bubbly on a hot afternoon is certainly one of life's more agreeable experiences,' said Joe, a few moments later. 'That sound advice we've just drunk to?—Is it a piece of Horatian wisdom?'

Bianca nodded. 'You can't have been *such* a dud at school, or you wouldn't have heard of Horace.'

'He didn't impinge on me at school. I came across him in the Legion where, most of the available reading matter being porn, one seizes any alternative, even translations of Latin poetry. That particular book was offered to me by an English botanist who came to Fuerteventura during my time there.'

He paused and, as she was about to question him about the island, he startled her by asking, 'Is your middle-aged swain still wooing you?'

'No, he isn't,' she answered shortly.

Joe's eyes glinted. 'Faint-hearted fellow. If I were laying siege to you, I shouldn't give up so easily.'

'Peter is a very modest man—not the type to consider himself irresistible.'

He grinned. 'And rightly so, if you've turned him down and don't mean to change your mind.'

'What does that prove? I'm sure there are plenty of women who would accept him eagerly, if he asked them.'

'Undoubtedly. Men with plenty of material assets never have to look far for eager females.'

'Or vice versa. Have you heard from your friend Mrs Russell since she went south?'

'No, I haven't. Are you implying that my relationship with Helen depends on her material assets?'

'You did once say that if you found a rich widow you would snap her up. Mrs Russell seems to fit the bill—and she's very attractive as well.'

'Were you jealous when you saw us together?'

'Jealous? No! What an absurd suggestion. Were you jealous when you saw me with Peter?'

'You were not alone with him. Had you been, I might have had some unkind thoughts about him.'

'I'm sure you were much too engrossed in your companion even to have noticed we were there if Lucy and I hadn't had to walk past your table.'

'Not so engrossed that I didn't see you scrutinising Helen but carefully avoiding catching my eye.'

'I was admiring her dress and her superb grooming. I felt you would probably rather we didn't intrude.'

Joe leaned towards her to refill her glass. Rather flustered by the turn of the conversation, she had drained it more quickly than she had intended.

'Your tact was unnecessary. Helen has far too much sense to be married for her money, and your nasty suspicions about my motives were quite unfounded,' he told her, with lazy amusement. 'My remark about a rich widow wasn't meant to be taken seriously. If the time ever comes when I feel an urge to marry, I'll do the supporting, or at least an equal share of it. But like you liberated girls, men like Rufus and myself who can cook and wash out a shirt aren't in pressing need of a mate except as a partner in bed, and one hears that wives are often less enthusiastic in that sphere than girl-friends.'

'I should think it depends on their husbands' prowess as lovers. Rufus is a bachelor only because the woman he loved was already married, and his generation didn't split up as lightly as ours does.'

Joe arched a sceptical eyebrow. 'Is that what he told you? I find it rather far-fetched. Human nature being what it is, I doubt if anyone nurses a hopeless passion for a lifetime as long as his has been. The truth is probably that he couldn't find a woman willing to share his kind of life. Most women are nesters. He's strictly a bird of passage.'

'I should think *Pago Pago* would make a most comfortable nest. There must be any number of women who like the idea of being free quite as much as men do, or who would accept a roving life because it was what their husband wanted and they wanted only to make him happy.'

'That's another idea which is too romantic by half,' he said. 'The woman who uncomplainingly follows her man to the ends of the earth, no matter how trying the conditions, is the rarest bird of them all. In my observation it's far more usual for the woman to set the life-style, and make the poor devil toe a line she has chosen. In fact, as often as not, the chaps who drop dead prematurely at forty or fifty weren't driving themselves. They were being driven by status-hungry wives.'

'That's a very disillusioned view of us.'

'Not so much disillusioned as without illusions in the first place. It's not quite the same.'

Bianca said quietly, 'I know true love and lasting happiness are not illusions because my parents had them, and would have them still, had they lived. I can believe that Rufus was faithful to one woman all his life—in mind if not always in body.'

'Let's finish the bottle, shall we?'

For the third time Joe filled her glass, and she wondered if this were a preliminary to making a pass at her. If it were, it had been an unnecessary preparation. The feeling of privacy given by being in a patch of shade in the brightest and hottest hour of the day, and his own powerful aura of attractive masculinity, were enough to make her inwardly responsive.

He had been lounging on one elbow, but now he remained sitting up and shifted closer to touch her ankle.

'It looks completely back to normal. Does it feel equally sound?'

'It was only a sprain.'

'Mm, but a bad one, and sometimes the ligaments take a surprisingly long time to recover their tone.' As he spoke, his fingers were gently stroking her instep and ankle.

Considering how strong his hands looked—as if he could crush an apple as easily as she could compress a grape—they could be incredibly gentle. Her leg was raised at the knee and, suddenly, Joe began to run his palm slowly up the back of her calf, watching her, as he did so, with the narrowed eyes and faintly smiling mouth which said as clearly as words that he knew its effect on her.

Bianca drew in her breath, her slim body braced for what she felt sure would be the volcanic effect of being caught close in Joe's powerful arms. But it didn't happen. For a second or two his hand lingered under her knee. Then he said, 'Time to cool off again, d'you think?' and, turning, sat with his back to her, looking at the sparkling sea.

She had only to stretch out her hand and touch him lightly on the shoulder-blade, and she knew he would turn to her again, and make what she had no doubt would be the most blissful love to her. Yet much as she wanted to make the gesture, something held her back and, one second before she had brought herself to the point of doing it, he rose to his feet with the single lithe upward movement of a man magnificently fit, and walked down into the water.

Her disappointment was sharp. And yet it was her own fault that he was now waist-deep in sea, instead of kissing her.

When, some hours later, they parted, he said, 'Shall we do the same thing tomorrow?'

This time she didn't hesitate. 'Yes, I'd love to, but let me bring the lunch.'

'Okay, you supply the food and I'll provide the plonk. *Hasta mañana.*'

The nights were becoming very hot and, waking some time in the small hours, Bianca went to the kitchen to fill a glass with aerated water from the refrigerator. Not feeling like going back to bed, she lit a spiral of an aromatic green substance to protect herself from mosquitoes, and took it on to the terrace where she sat in the moonlight, sipping the icy water and watching the distant sierras, and thinking over the afternoon.

'Seize today,' she had toasted, sipping champagne. But when today had offered her the chance to feel round her the arms of a man whom she found compellingly attractive, she had not seized it. Why had she rejected the opportunity or, if not precisely rejected it, missed it by being uncertain?

Not, as she was aware, that Joe had depended on her tacit permission to kiss her. There were men who with outward assurance disguised their innate diffidence. But he was not one of them. She felt sure that his self-confidence went all the way through to the core of him.

What he wanted from women he would take, and they would enjoy his taking it, because he was that kind of man; and because that was how, fundamentally, a woman wanted a man to be. Not to ride rough-shod over her like the tyrannical husbands of Victorian times, but still to be master, if not in all things, at least in their love relationship. A suppliant man, like poor Peter, was as unexciting as cold porridge, thought Bianca. 'A faint-hearted fellow' Joe had called him, smiling at her with a predatory gleam in his tawny eyes. To remember his touch on her leg made her shiver with mingled apprehension and anticipation. What might he do to her tomorrow?

CHAPTER FIVE

THE next day they had lunch on board, and Joe asked, 'Will your job in London still be open when you feel you're free to go back?'

'No, but I can find another. The techniques of research can be applied in many ways. The television companies employ researchers for most programmes, and quite a few famous authors don't dig out their facts, they have all the groundwork done for them by people like me. I'd prefer to get back into genealogy, but if I can't I'm not afraid of being jobless. What about your future plans? Have you any?'

Today he had rigged the awning over the cockpit, and set up a collapsible table at which they were sitting opposite each other, eating a quiche Lorraine which Bianca had reheated in his oven, with a mixed salad, and a bottle of mellow old *vino rancio* with the flowery flavour which she preferred to a dry wine.

Joe put down his knife and fork and twisted the stem of his wine-glass, his eyes on the crimson liquid, his expression thoughtful.

'No very firm ones,' he said. 'I thought I might take a look at the Caribbean, and from there go on to the Pacific. But I like it here for the present.'

He raised his eyes to meet hers, and she wondered, with a pang of unease, if the rather inscrutable look he gave her could, by someone more experienced than herself, be construed to mean that she was one of the reasons he was content to linger on the Costa Blanca; and that, metaphorically, having added her scalp to those already on his belt, he would be ready to move on.

'Why that wary look?' he asked, reading her mind much more closely than she could read his.

Before she could answer, he went on, 'I don't think you approve of men like me, do you, Bianca? It strikes you as rather suspect for a man to cut free from the herd, and live life without any pattern, hm?'

'Not suspect—enviable. I should love to be free to go where I pleased and do as I liked. As a successful artist, my mother had that kind of freedom, although while my father was alive she went wherever he went. Fortunately most of the places where he had to go were ones she liked, such as Italy. For a time, after his death, she did travel with total freedom, but she said it was often terribly lonely being in some glorious part of the world but having no one to share the experience. It was partly loneliness and partly misguided pity which made her marry Ben. What I should like——' she stopped short.

'Yes, go on—what would you like?'

She had nearly said, 'I should like to be free because my husband was a free man.' She could have said it to Rufus, but she couldn't to Joe. It sounded too much as if she had designs on him, and that wasn't true. She was ready to fall in love with him, but still on the brink, still capable of stepping back. Her state of mind was perfectly expressed by one of her mother's favourite records, *When I Fall In Love*, a long-ago hit now only occasionally revived on the radio, and a song which Bianca had not played since Carla's death because she felt it would be too poignant a reminder of the warm, glowing personality whose absence she still felt deeply.

Now, as the words of the song came into her mind, she realised that, like the best poems, the best songs held truths which one didn't always appreciate until one experienced the emotion they expressed. At some time the writer of that song must have felt exactly as she did now: determined not to fall in love unless it was for ever, and waiting for the moment when the other person showed a sign of feeling the same way.

She closed the rather long pause by saying, 'What I should like is to have what my parents enjoyed; separate professional lives, and a shared private life. But that's very hard to achieve. So often people's jobs conflict instead of meshing. Not that I have a career in the true sense. It's an interesting way of earning my living, not a vocation.'

For their pudding she had made a French fruit tart and whipped some cream to serve with it. Watching him cut two large slices, she asked, 'Do you visualise doing what you do now for the rest of your life?'

'Probably, but until recently I didn't give much thought to the future.'

'And now you do?'

'Not a great deal, but there are nights when I should prefer to be earning my living by day, and not in a fug of cigarette smoke. I'm by nature an early riser.'

'Me, too. I should hate to have to miss the first hour after sunrise. Not that I used to get up early in London. But here, surrounded by mountains, first thing in the morning is heavenly, and so are the beaches.'

Joe had stopped eating the tart to look at her with the sudden intensity which she always found slightly unnerving.

'What is it?' she asked, after some moments. 'Why are you looking at me like that?'

'You're very pleasing to the eye, especially when you're speaking of something enjoyable. It makes you very nearly beautiful.' Two creases formed down his cheeks as his mouth began to smile. 'Not quite, but nearly.'

'You overwhelm me,' she said lightly.

'Not at the moment, but I think I could if I wanted to—and if you wanted me to.'

Bianca looked down at her plate. 'I—I'm not really sure what you mean by that.'

'But you have an uneasy suspicion that it might be something improper?' His tone was both teasing and caressing.

She cut into her slice of tart with the edge of her fork but, having separated a mouthful, pushed it round her plate as a pretext for keeping her glance averted.

'Do I seem so extremely prim to you?' she asked.

'Not at all. Judging by your instinctive response when I kissed you, under the surface you're anything but prim,' he replied. 'At the same time you give the impression of having a lot of potential, but not a great deal of practice—not much more than Lucy, perhaps.'

'Perhaps . . . perhaps not,' she answered.

'The other day Rufus showed me a poem to a girl with your name. I wonder if I can remember it?'

His hand came across the table and took her by the chin, and made her look at him.

'It was a poem by Robert Herrick. I can remember one verse—rather appropriate in the circumstances.'

Her throat had tightened. Her 'Really?' came out rather hoarsely.

'Yes, very appropriate.' His fingers still held her chin, and his tiger's eyes gleamed with amusement. He began to recite the verse to her.

> 'Bianca, let
> Me pay the debt
> I owe thee for a kiss
> Thou lent'st to me,
> And I to thee
> Will render ten for this.'

Her eyelashes fluttered. No one had ever blandished her with poetry before, and his deep voice and glinting eyes gave the words an impact which made her tingle.

'I didn't lend it. You took it,' she told him unsteadily.

'All the more reason for me to repay it with interest.' A pause. 'Unless you would rather I didn't?'

With an effort she pulled herself together. 'I'm sure *you* have boundless experience, Joe, so you ought to know that the answer to "Can I kiss you?" is always No.' She put her fingers on his wrist to make him release her chin. 'Don't you like the tart? Are you going to leave it?' she asked, in her most prosaic tone.

'Not likely,' he said, at once, and finished his helping with the relish with which he had begun it.

He would be a nice person to cook for, she thought, watching him.

Presently, while they were washing up, he said, 'Next time I shan't ask.'

She looked sideways at him. She was washing and he was wiping, the top of his head having only a few inches' clearance in the small but well-equipped galley.

She wondered suddenly if he could take teasing as well as he gave it. Straight-faced, she asked, 'Have you ever seen the American tee-shirt with the big, smiling toad, licking his lips, and the inscription "Before you meet the Handsome Prince, you've gotta kiss a lot of Toads"?'

Joe laughed, showing his sound white teeth. 'Are you telling me I'm a toad, girl?'

'I don't know. Perhaps you're a prince.' She put the last dish on the drainer. 'But somehow I shouldn't think so.'

For once she had him checkmated, and he took it in good part. But still, in a way, the joke was on her. For if Joe was a toad, she knew she would rather have him than a dozen princes.

Every afternoon for a week he took her sailing and taught her the rudiments of his own expert seamanship. And every evening, half an hour before he went to work, he took her ashore and shook hands with a smile in his eyes because he had still not kissed her, and he knew—she felt certain he knew—that his patience increased her impatience.

In the end he took her by surprise; catching hold of her at a moment when she was peering over the side, watching a particularly large parachute-shaped jellyfish and, for a change, completely relaxed and intent on the creature in the water.

When Joe took hold of her shoulders, drew her upright and turned her to face him she was so far off guard that, by the time she realised what he intended to do, he was already doing it; pressing his mouth firmly on hers in a kiss which went on and on, like an endless dive into fathomless depths of pleasure from which she wanted never to surface.

He kissed her in all the ways she had known before, and in others she had not experienced and, presently, while he kissed her he began to stroke her brown skin, nearly all of it bare to his touch. His exploring fingers caressed the line of her spine made concave by her arched throat and backward-bent head. Then one palm curved over her hip while his other hand spanned the base of her shoulder-blades to press her more closely against him. His skin was cool from the sea in which, a few moments before, he had still been swimming. But she felt the fire burning inside him as he stopped gently nibbling her ears and reclaimed her soft, parted lips in another long, dizzying kiss which robbed her of all sane thought. For a while she became a mindless being conscious of nothing but the pulsating delight of being held by a man whose power to excite her senses was as masterly as his handling of his boat.

It was not until she felt him beginning to untie the

strings of the halter of her bikini that she put up any resistance.

'My darling girl, who's to see?' he murmured, in an amused voice. 'But if you'd rather we went below ...'

He released his hold on her waist and, taking her by the hand, began to step down into the day cabin.

Unable to free her fingers from his strong clasp, Bianca grabbed at the helm as an aid to staying where she was.

'You're going too fast for me, Joe.'

He paused, and lifted an eyebrow. 'Am I? I thought I'd been going exceptionally slowly.'

'Up to now, yes,' she agreed. 'But now you're going *much* too fast.'

'There's no need to cling to the wheel. I shan't drag you down by your hair if you won't come willingly. But a moment ago you seemed willing.'

'To kiss you, yes ... but not to jump into bed. I—I told you that at the beginning.'

'Yes, I remember. You said your life was already difficult, and you weren't in the market for a casual affair. I'm not suggesting we should have one.' He moved close enough to touch her lightly on the cheek. For a heart-stopping moment the gentleness of his expression made her think he was going to say next, 'I love you. I want you to marry me.'

Instead of which, what he said was, 'These afternoons are very pleasant, but they're not enough. I'd like to have breakfast with you, and to know you'll be here when I finish work at the restaurant. Come and live on board and be happy. You can still keep an eye on the other two, but they'll be less of a burden on you.'

He bent his head and, with his lips to her cheek, said in a low, husky voice, 'I want you very much, Bianca.'

She wanted to melt into his arms, to cling to his hard

strong body, and surrender her own without restraint.

'No, I can't ... I can't, Joe,' she whispered.

He began to kiss her again and, knowing it was madness, she did not immediately resist. But this time not only was her own pleasure marred by the fear of being swept away, but she knew it was unfair to him. It had to be all or nothing ... so it had to be nothing.

As she drew free, he said, 'Why not, Bianca? You want this as much as I do. You're hungry for love. Why not admit it?'

She said, with attempted lightness, 'Sometimes I'm hungry for a second slice of toast and honey for breakfast, but one can't give way to every impulse. If one does, one gets fat.'

'Love improves women's looks.'

'Happiness may—but I shouldn't be happy being the girl who lives with Joe Crawford. It's just not my style.'

He didn't argue with her. He didn't react in any of the ways she had heard of men behaving in these circumstances.

He said merely, and perfectly pleasantly, 'All right, if that's how you feel. But if you should change your mind, the offer will still be open. Shall we have another swim?'

For the rest of the afternoon it was as if nothing had happened between them. Bianca would not have believed that any man would take a refusal in such a civilised way; although, of course, it had not been a rebuff. She had given him plenty of evidence that she found him compellingly attractive, and had turned down his proposition on a conscientious objection, not because of aversion or indifference.

When the time came to sail back to harbour, she sat on the foredeck, her arms round her updrawn knees, while Joe remained at the helm and Fred stood in the bows. For the most part they glided smoothly over the glittering water, but now and again crossing the wake of another craft, La Libertad bounced and Bianca noticed with amusement how adeptly the dog adjusted his balance to the movement. However, most of the way back her mood was sombre and regretful because she knew it was the end of her sailing lessons and of a very happy interlude.

There were always people on the quay; Spanish men and boys fishing, foreign holidaymakers strolling, boat people coming and going. As La Libertad returned to her berth, Bianca noticed but failed to recognise a fair-haired man watching their return from his seat on top of the sea wall.

It was not until she was going ashore in the dinghy that, as the man stood up and removed his sun-glasses, she gave a startled exclamation which made Joe glance at her enquiringly.

'What's the matter?'

'It's Michael ... an old friend of mine.' As Michael came down the stairs to quay level, she raised her voice to call, 'What are you doing here?'

He stood at the top of the landing steps as she climbed them. 'Hello, Bianca. How are you? Need I ask? You look like an ad. for Ambre Solaire.' His glance shifted to Joe who had followed her up the steps.

She introduced them. 'Michael Leigh ... Joe Crawford.'

As the two men shook hands she saw Michael flinch slightly as Joe's brown hand gripped his paler one. Probably Joe modified his clasp when he shook hands with women, but not with men. Instinctively, she knew they would not like each other.

'When did you arrive? Are you just passing through?' she asked Michael.

'I'm on what's known as a fly-drive holiday. It includes the flight and a car, but no accommodation. I arrived at

Alicante yesterday, spent the night there and moved on this morning. Your stepfather told me where I might find you.'

'I see.' Bianca found it difficult to know what to say next.

Before she could think of anything, Joe said, 'I must get changed and go to work. I hope you enjoy your visit, Leigh. "*Diós*, Bianca.'

'"*Diós*,' she echoed.

As he propelled himself back to *La Libertad*, she and Michael began to walk along the quay.

'Striking chap, your sailing companion,' he remarked. 'What is he? A restaurateur?'

'No, he plays the piano in a restaurant.'

'Really? How come?'

'What do you mean—how come?'

'It can't be his regular living.'

'I believe so. Why not?'

'It's an odd occupation, don't you think? The boat can't be his, presumably?'

'As far as I know it is.'

'A boat of that size would cost twenty-five thousand or more. It's a rich person's toy.'

'It's not Joe's toy, it's his home. I believe in the past he's made a living by chartering. Most of the boats along the public quay are their owners' homes, not merely pleasure craft. You find more of those at the yacht club on the opposite side of the harbour. The members are mainly Spanish people who live in Valencia and come down here at weekends, plus a sprinkling of wealthy Germans and Hollanders. Or so I've been told. I've never actually been in the club.'

She went on talking about the town, turning her mind and Michael's away from Joe, shutting out all thought of him until she could be alone.

To her surprise Ben, who usually spent this time of day in the village bar, was at home when they returned. For the first time in weeks he had set up his easel on the veranda, and was dashing off the view of the harbour which, when he had been painting more regularly had been one of his most successful sellers; and which, having done it so often, he could paint without reference to sketch notes.

Bianca left the two men chatting while she went to the kitchen to see about supper. On the table she found a note from Lucy who had come home at lunch time but was spending the evening with a girl friend.

'It will be a scratch meal, I'm afraid, Michael,' said Bianca when, some time later, she took dishes of almonds and olives out to the men. 'How long does your holiday last, and what's your itinerary?'

'Ten days, but I have no itinerary. I came to see you,' he replied.

She felt she must be misinterpreting his tone and the expression in his eyes. He had read Carla Dawson's obituary notice in *The Times* and written a letter of condolence which Bianca had felt obliged to acknowledge. But it had been their only communication since the—at the time— shattering letter announcing the existence of another girl in his life. Yet now he seemed to be looking at her as if there had never been a rift between them.

'Have you fixed a room for the night?' she asked. 'At this time of year, when everywhere's heavily booked, it pays to register as early in the day as possible.'

'No, I haven't organised that yet, but I'm sure I shall find a bed somewhere. Which hotel is the best?' he enquired.

'I don't know. I've never stayed in any of them.'

Ben said, 'No need to go to an hotel, old boy. We can put you up here. Can't give you a room to yourself—there are only three bedrooms—but you're welcome to sleep on the sofa-bed, isn't he, Bianca?'

She masked her dismay, and answered, 'I think he would be more comfortable in an hotel.'

'I wasn't last night, in Alicante,' said Michael. 'My room reminded me of that *New Yorker* cartoon with a house agent telling some buyers, "Yes, the walls *are* paper-thin. But you'll find your neighbour possesses a rapier-like wit, full of amusing double entendres and profusely studded with literary allusions".'

Ben guffawed, and Bianca had to smile, but her heart sank as Michael accepted her stepfather's offer. Too late, she realised that she should have made him register at an hotel before bringing him to the Casa Mimosa. Probably Ben imagined he was being helpful, but it was rather brash of Michael to accept the invitation when he must have sensed that she did not wish him to stay.

After supper, while the two men chatted, she cleared the table, washed the dishes and made up the sofa-bed. From where he was sitting on the veranda, Michael could see her doing this last, but he didn't offer to help. She had always known that he was an extremely undomesticated man, partly because he had a widowed mother who delighted in doing his laundry when he went home for weekends, and who had even been known to come to London for a day's shopping and spent half of it tidying his flat. At the time Bianca had not given much thought to that aspect of his character. But now, in the light of her association with Joe and Rufus, she found his incompetence irritating.

Strange, that a man who once had been all-important to her should now be an unwelcome encumbrance. Would the time come when her present feeling for Joe would suffer a similar alteration? Was she seeing him at the moment through the distorting lens of physical infatuation?

The realisation that she was thinking about him, when she had resolved not to do so until she was alone, made her give herself a mental shake.

When she rejoined the men, Ben suggested, 'How about a stroll as far as the bar?'

'I'll stay here, if you don't mind,' said Bianca, as Michael waited for her reaction to this suggestion. 'I find the village bar too noisy, but if you'd like to see some local life, don't mind me, Michael.'

'Is there somewhere quieter we could go?'

'Not unless we go back into town, which is rather far for a drink. To be honest, I could do with an early night. Had we known you were coming——' She left the sentence in the air.

'I'm off to Juanita's,' said Ben. 'If I don't see you again tonight, Leigh, we'll meet at breakfast. 'Night, Bianca.' With a wave of his hand, he left them.

'Nice chap, your stepfather,' said Michael.

'Yes,' she agreed. She saw no reason to disillusion him, and hoped Ben would not. 'You should have gone with him, Michael. Juanita's is fun, the first time or two.'

'I'd much rather stay with you. You said you needed an early night. Do you live it up a great deal here?'

'Not excessively. One *could* go to a party every night, and some people do, but I don't.'

'I thought you'd have come back to London by now. But you like it in Spain, apparently?'

'Yes, I do. Who wouldn't?' she answered, with a gesture which encompassed the moonlit garden, the dark outlines of the far sierras, and the twinkling golden lights of the villas on the nearer hillsides. 'I was always a country person, really, although my job was in London.'

'But here you're a lady of leisure, I gather?'

'Oh, no—not at all. I have a part-time job in the morning, and running the house occupies a good deal of time. Can I give you some more wine, or would you prefer something else now?'

'Wine would be fine.' As she refilled his glass, he said, 'I can guess what you've been thinking—that I've got a hell of a nerve to turn up like this.'

'I admit I was surprised to see you. What happened to the girl you wrote to me about?'

'It didn't work out. It was a mistake from the outset: one of those rebound things which should never have happened and wouldn't—had ours been a stronger relationship. But although you once told me you loved me, you always kept me at arm's length, and although I understood your mother's claim on you, I felt I had none at all. Leaving me didn't seem to worry you.'

'No, it didn't *worry* me,' she agreed. 'At the time I hoped a separation would make you realise ... would make you want the kind of permanent, wholehearted commitment which I wanted—then. Instead you turned to someone else, proving that you were right, and I was wrong about us. What we felt for each other was not strong enough to last for ever.'

'On the contrary, it has proved to me that *you* were right. I was a fool not to realise what a treasure I had in you, Bianca. Now that I've come to my senses, I suppose it's too late? You're involved with someone else, I imagine?'

'I'm more involved with family problems than with any personal relationships. My stepsister can be rather a handful ... Ah, here she comes now.'

With considerable relief, Bianca caught the sound of Lucy's moped.

There had been a time when Lucy, if she had suspected that a man wanted to be alone with Bianca, would deliberately have played gooseberry. Now that she no longer had the chip on her shoulder which had made her delight in being tiresome, she would have gone to her room after only a brief conversation with Bianca's visitor. However, on the pretext of helping her to organise a snack, Bianca was able to ask her not to leave them alone together.

'Why not?' asked Lucy, in an undertone.

'I'll explain tomorrow,' Bianca muttered.

Much later, lying in bed, she wondered where she would be now if she had not resisted Joe. Probably *La Libertad* would still be moored in the bay where he had kissed her, and either they would be sharing his bunk or, if it was too narrow for comfort, lying under the stars on a bed made from the squabs from the saloon. On land at this time of year, the nights were often too hot, but at sea, even not far from shore, the air would be fresher, and there would be no insects—this thought as a familiar whining sound told her that, although her open window was screened by a fine nylon mesh, at some time during the day a mosquito had flown in, and would have to be dealt with if she wanted to avoid waking up with at least one inflamed bite.

'I see what you meant about having family problems,' said Michael, the following morning, as he drove her to town.

She knew he had been kept awake for a long time by what, from her room, had sounded like one of Ben's most maudlin monologues.

'That's why you can't stay with us, Michael. It's not that I want to seem inhospitable, but it's embarrassing for Lucy.'

'Okay, I'll find an hotel room.'

'If you can,' she said doubtfully.

'They won't all be full,' he said confidently.

'Good morning, m'dear, Joe tells me you have a friend

from England visiting you. There's no need to continue your work for me if you'd like to be free to show him around and enjoy yourself,' said Rufus, when he came to ferry her on board.

It was on the tip of her tongue to answer that Michael was an unwelcome visitor whom she hoped to discourage from staying long. But, in case it should get back to Joe, she thought better of this reply, and said only that Michael did not need her company all day, and she preferred to carry on as usual.

Joe who often, although not invariably, stopped by for a beer during the morning, did not do so, and Bianca wondered if this was deliberate or if it was merely that something had prevented him from joining them.

The last thing she expected was to find, at the end of the morning, that Michael was waiting for her neither on the sea wall nor strolling about on the quay, but was drinking chilled lager in the cockpit of *La Libertad*. On joining him there, she was even more disconcerted to be told that Joe was taking them sailing, and Michael had been to the market and organised a picnic.

'Perhaps Rufus would like to come along,' said Joe, meeting her wary glance with a bland expression which gave her no clue to his motive for being friendly towards Michael when she felt they had nothing in common.

'He's a little bit evasive, our host,' said Michael, keeping his voice down, when Joe had left them to go and invite Rufus to make up a foursome. 'I wonder why?'

'What did you ask him that he avoided answering?'

'Only the usual questions which one does ask people to form some idea of their place in the scheme of things. But I now know as little about Crawford's background as I did when we started chatting over an hour ago.'

'I'm not sure I don't prefer people who are reserved

to those who pour out their entire and often extremely dull life story as soon as one meets them,' said Bianca.

She took off her dark glasses and, with closed eyes, lifted her face to the sun, remembering with regret the short-lived idyll of those sailing days alone with Joe, when the attraction between them was still undeclared.

Michael's touch on her skin startled and displeased her. He stroked the slim length of her forearm, his hand coming to rest over hers which was spread on the lid of the locker on which they were sitting.

She slid her hand away. 'Don't, Michael. I told you last night, we can't revive the past.'

'I'm not going to accept that—not yet. I have eight days to try to make you change your mind, and——' Seeing Joe coming back, he broke off.

How ironic, she thought, that the two men who had no power over her—one of them never, and one no longer —should be so much more persistent than the man whose dangerously potent magnetism she had only just managed to resist, and who had accepted her resistance with such unexpected good grace. But that had been only yesterday, and perhaps it was part of his technique to take the first reverse lightly because he was sure that she wouldn't always resist him.

She thought it unlikely that Joe, when he went to ask Rufus to join them, had suggested to the old man that he should engage Michael's attention while he, Joe, concentrated on her. But that was the way it turned out. Not that Joe could undermine her defences to any serious extent while the others were present. But every happy moment she spent with him made it harder to hold to her determination not to have anything more to do with him.

Michael, she found, when they moored for lunch, was

an indifferent swimmer, and did not much like the water
except as a means of cooling off. His ungraceful style was
all the more noticeable while he was in the company of
Joe who swam like a merman, and the discovery of this
hitherto unknown aspect of Michael made her realise that
one could know a man for a long time and still remain
ignorant of a fundamental incompatability. For her to
marry a man who did not love the sea as she did would
have been almost as hard as marrying someone who found
no pleasure in reading, music or art.

She knew Joe liked reading and music, but was he interested in paintings? Would it have bored him to wander
round the several floors of the Bellas Artes museum of
art in Valencia, as she and her mother had often done
when, in the time before Carla's illness, they had gone to
the city to shop?

She remembered that he had heard of her mother, and
mentioned her to Mrs Russell, but that did not mean he
was a lover of art.

'Do you know much about paintings, Joe?' she asked,
while Rufus was explaining to Michael his reasons for
writing his memoirs.

'Not a great deal. I know what I like.'

He discussed his taste at some length, showing a know-
ledge of certain art forms, such as marine paintings, which
could only have been acquired by someone with a stronger
than average interest in the subject.

'Why did you ask?' he enquired.

'Oh, merely idle curiosity.' His question made her realise
that she should not be feeling pleased to find that this
was yet another area in which they had a rapport.

She did not see Joe again until the last night of Michael's
stay when, somewhat to her surprise and greatly to her
relief, he suggested they should make up a foursome with

a man he had met at his hotel whom he thought would be a valuable contact.

'I'm afraid you'll find his girl-friend rather bird-brained, but Rolf is an up-and-coming man in TV, on the production side, and he could put a lot of work my way if I can foster our acquaintance,' he explained.

Even before she met him Bianca found the idea of cultivating someone for their usefulness vaguely distasteful. When Michael introduced her and Rolf she found it even more objectionable. For even before Rolf gave her an undressing look as they shook hands, she took him for a posturing phoney to whom she could never toady, no matter how powerful his influence.

His girl-friend she did not dislike. Patti might not be very intelligent, but she was as friendly as a puppy, and as Bianca enjoyed the company of her own sex, and did not disdain to chat about clothes and make-up when the occasion demanded, she did not find the other girl as boring as Michael had forecast.

Obviously Patti was accustomed to being ignored by Rolf whenever he had another man to talk to, and—although she regretted it later—during dinner it amused Bianca to play up to Rolf's assumption that she was another dim and amenable female who needed only to be wined, dined, and tossed an occasional remark to be content.

To the two or three remarks he addressed to her, she responded with wide-eyed looks and replies of a consummate banality which made Michael glance uneasily at her.

Joe, being a more percipient man, would have seen through it and grinned, she thought. Except that Joe would never feel it was necessary to lick anyone's boots, least of all the high-heeled white patent cowboy boots of a man like Rolf who took his trendiness to a point which, to her, indicated that beneath the bounce lay a deep-seated lack of confidence in his own personality.

Having eaten, they discussed where to go next. Rolf, who had lighted an ostentatiously large cigar and was puffing clouds of smoke regardless of whether he might be impairing the enjoyment of people still eating, said, 'You live here, Bianca. You must know all the best places.'

Before she could answer, Patti said, 'I know a good club to go to—a girl I met at the hairdresser's this morning was telling me about it. She said it was *the* place to dance here. The others are all ordinary discos, but this one has a live group and a good atmosphere.'

'Ah, but do you remember the name of it?' Rolf enquired, in the patronising tone which seemed to be how he spoke to her all the time.

'Of course I do, Rolfie.' Patti seemed unaware of being patronised, and equally unaware that he didn't like her calling him Rolfie. 'It's called El Delfin. It means *The* Dolphin,' she explained.

'Quite the little polyglot, our Patti,' Rolf murmured, smirking.

Bianca felt like kicking him on Patti's behalf. She said, 'I don't think you'd find El Delfin very special if you're used to the best in London.' This was a mild dig at Rolf who, earlier, had been trying to impress them by mentioning various de luxe hotels and nightclubs of which, so he implied, he was an habitué. 'There's an open air place which isn't bad——'

'El Delfin is air-conditioned,' Patti broke in. 'It won't be too hot.'

'We'll try it. If we don't like it we can always move on,' said Michael.

Bianca had never been in the nightclub part of El Delfin and she hoped that, like many such places, it would be too dimly lit for Joe to notice her.

In the restaurant he played the piano with his back to the room. But in the nightclub the instrument was set sideways on the dais. He had only to turn his head to see who was at the tables surrounding the small circle of dance floor.

When they arrived, the other musicians were taking a break and Joe was playing on his own. As Michael and his party followed a waiter to a table at the back of the room, she recognised the distinctive opening bars of the song she had asked him to play the first time they met. Could it be a coincidence merely that he had switched from a tune she didn't know to one which had always been a favourite of hers, and which now had a special significance?

'I like this number, but I can't remember what it's called,' said Patti, as they sat down.

'*A Man And A Woman*,' Bianca told her. Covertly, she glanced towards the dais. Joe was not looking in their direction, so probably it was just a coincidence.

Presently the rest of the group returned. They played to a pattern of two or three hot numbers, then something slow and sexy.

Rolf, being an exhibitionist, was a better dancer than Michael. But the first time Bianca danced to one of the slow numbers with him, she found he was one of those tiresome men who went in for unwelcome fondling. She did not want to have his cheek pressed to hers, and to feel his hand straying over her hips, but on an overcrowded floor it was difficult to draw away. Short of saying bluntly, 'Please stop it,' there seemed to be little she could do but submit for the present, and avoid another slow dance with him.

A brown hand fell on his shoulder.

'May I have the rest of this dance, Bianca?'

'Do you mind, Rolf? Joe's an old friend.'

In spite of her earlier hope that he would not see her, she could not help feeling relieved at being rescued from an embrace which she had found anything but pleasant, and taken lightly into the arms of the man who, however he might upset her in other ways, could never be physically repellent to her.

'Who is *that* character?' asked Joe, when Rolf was on his way back to the table.

'Someone Michael met at his hotel.'

'Michael may find him congenial. You didn't look as if you did.'

'No, I quite like his poor little girl-friend, but he's a horrid piece of work. I don't think Michael actually *likes* him, but he might be useful to him professionally.'

Joe looked down and lifted both eyebrows. 'And for that he'll watch you being pawed?'

'He's dancing with Patti, I think. Probably he didn't notice.'

'I did,' he said, in a dry tone. 'And if anyone's going to make love to you on the dance floor, it's going to be me—not that creep.'

He drew her to him, pressing her closer and closer until they were locked together from shoulder to knee.

'Oh, Joe ... it's not fair,' she protested faintly.

'You don't like it?' he murmured in her ear.

Bianca didn't answer. To deny that she liked it was impossible when he must be able to feel the excited beating of her heart, the instinctive yielding of her body.

'Are you allowed to leave the piano?' she asked.

'The last time I did was for Lucy's benefit. I don't think they'll fire me.'

She suspected him of asking the guitarist who was the group's leader to make the number last longer than would have been normal. It seemed to go on for ever, and every moment in his arms made her more deeply conscious that probably never in her life would she meet another man like him. In every way except one they seemed to be perfect for each other; but she wanted total commitment, and he wasn't ready for that, and perhaps never would be.

'So your friend Michael isn't staying at the house now?'

'No.' She didn't want to talk; only to commit to memory the feel of his lean dark cheek which, because she was wearing high heels, he could press against hers without bending as he had bent to kiss her when she was barefoot and next to naked. Not that her thin evening dress offered much more protection from the hand on the small of her back with the thumb moving on her bare skin. Her other hand he was holding flat to his chest which felt like the warm, hard surface of a wall of rock. Because they were locked together, the back of his hand was resting against her right breast, with his knuckles above the low neckline in a contact which burned her like a brand.

'I take it he's an old flame?'

'You could say that, yes.'

'Did he ever light your fire, Bianca?'

'At one time I was very fond of him,' she admitted.

'I think he's wasting his time now.'

'Do you? He wants to marry me.'

He drew back enough to look at her. 'You're a self-confessed idealist. You wouldn't marry for anything less than love, and if you loved him you wouldn't be soft in my arms. You'd be as rigid as you were with the bearded chap.'

She tried to stiffen and withdraw, as she had with Rolf, but the hand on her back increased its pressure and after a moment she gave up her sham resistance and surrendered to the unwise delight—which could only last a little longer

—of being, as he himself put it, soft in his arms.

When the music came to an end, he released her with a reluctance which was balm to her self-esteem if it did not ease her common sense. At least she was not the victim of a one-sided infatuation, if infatuation was what this was. Joe cared enough for her to resent Rolf's manner of dancing with her and, all the time they were on the floor, she had felt his leashed passion for her.

He took her back to the table and there bowed over her hand. 'Thank you, Bianca. Goodnight.'

He did not wait to be introduced to the others, but strode back to his place on the dais.

'Mm ... dishy! Spanish?' asked Patti, as Bianca sat down next to her.

'No, English.'

'He sounded it, but he looks rather Spanish, doesn't he? Except for being so much taller than they usually are. I'd adore to have my hand kissed like that,' said Patti, with a wriggle and a giggle which made Bianca smile and Rolf glower.

What a humourless twit the man is, she thought. If the girl wants her hand kissed, why doesn't he kiss it for her? She glanced at Michael who was looking equally unamused.

Later, driving her home, he said to her, 'I don't know how Rolf can stand that girl's inane chatter. She may have a splendid body, but almost nothing between the ears.'

'No, or she wouldn't waste herself on a horror like Rolf. What a really appalling man, Michael.'

'Appalling? He's a brilliant director.'

'Yes, I can imagine the kind of plays he directs. Either sick or sex-ridden, or both. Not a normal human being to be seen.'

'You don't seem to object to sex when it takes the form of a Latin-looking hunk of muscle with a talent for kissing women's hands and an IQ which is probably even lower than Patti's,' he retorted sourly. 'If I hadn't seen it with my own eyes, I wouldn't have believed a girl as intelligent as yourself could fall for a type like that. But you have fallen for him, haven't you?'

'Yes, I think I have,' she admitted.

'I knew it the moment I saw you with him. For God's sake, Bianca, be sensible. I grant you that Crawford has charm, but you don't think he's serious about you, do you?'

'It depends what you mean by serious. He wants me to live with him—as you did at one time, Michael,' she reminded him mildly.

He pulled the car off the road and turned to face her.

'But now I want you to marry me.' He took her in his arms and kissed her.

It was a curious sensation to be embraced by a man she had loved, or thought she had loved, and to remain unmoved except by wonder that, for many nights after his letter breaking things off between them, she had cried herself to sleep. Perhaps it had been partly her profound distress about her mother which had made the ending of their love affair seem a heartbreak from which she would never fully recover.

At first Michael seemed unaware that she was submitting to his kiss but not responding to it. Then her lack of reaction seemed to enrage him. He began to kiss and caress her in a way which she now found unbearable. She had to break free, protesting.

'You've slept with him, haven't you?' he said bitterly. 'You always kept me at arm's length, but you've slept with him, damn him. Oh God! Why are women such fools? I want to *marry* you, Bianca.'

'You didn't then, Michael—not then.'

'I do now.' He tried to recapture her, but she fended him off, saying angrily, 'Please take me home.' There was no doubt in her mind that any relationship with Joe, however irregular, was preferable to marriage to Michael.

They parted with superficial civility, but the evening had been an unpleasant ending to a difficult interlude, and she felt the blame was not all his. She should have been firmer, and sent him away at the outset.

CHAPTER SIX

ABOUT a week later, early in the evening, before Lucy had come home from work, Bianca was washing a lettuce when she heard the slam of a car door and, soon afterwards, someone tugging the string of the goat bell which served as their door bell.

Wondering who it could be, for Peter would have called, 'Are you there?' and walked in, she dried her wet hands and went through the living-room to find out.

To her dismay—she refused to admit to the sudden glow of warmth underlying the dismay—she found Joe standing on the terrace.

'Hello, Bianca. How are you?'

'Fine, thanks. What brings you here?' Deliberately, she made her tone polite but unwelcoming.

'I came to tell you not to go to the harbour tomorrow. Rufus won't be around—he was taken ill this afternoon. Now he's in the clinic and likely to be there for some time.'

'Taken ill?' she exclaimed. 'He seemed perfectly all right when I left him. What happened?'

'He appears to have had a heart attack. Fortunately I called on him a few minutes after it happened, and the best thing to do seemed to be to borrow a car and take him straight to the clinic. It may not be true, but I've heard that calling an ambulance can be a long-winded process here.'

'I don't know about the ambulance service, but I do know that some Spanish hospitals are run on quite different lines

119

from English ones. They don't always have nursing auxili-
aries to attend to the general care of patients. Here, all that
is often done by relations, and poor Rufus has no relations.'

'I can look after him,' said Joe.

'How can you? He'll need someone there all the time,
or most of it, and you can't be playing half the night and
be at the clinic in time to give Rufus his breakfast. But
don't worry: I'll look after him, and you can relieve me
for a few hours in the afternoon.'

He frowned. 'I don't think that's a good idea. You've
already had to cope with your mother's illness, and the fact
that you've been helping Rufus with his memoirs recently
doesn't put you under any obligation to tackle this situation.'

'I know it doesn't, but I happen to like Rufus, and one
of these days I may be old and ill myself, and dependent
on my friends to rally round me.'

'In that case we'll do it between us.'

In the first phase of Rufus's illness, Joe proved to be as
capable as Bianca in looking after the old man's non-
medical needs. Indeed he spent longer hours at the clinic
than she did, and undertook all the necessary tasks with the
same calm competence with which he handled his boat. It
was he who gave Rufus blanket baths; he who spent the
night with him.

When she protested about this, saying that she was in a
better position to undertake night duties, Joe told her
firmly not to argue. He had arranged to continue to play at
the restaurant until half past ten at night, but not to play
in the nightclub while Rufus's condition gave cause for
concern.

'But surely they'll dock your pay. How will you manage?'
she objected.

'Don't worry, I'm not going to starve. I'm probably better at cat-napping than you are. I can sleep anywhere, and wake up alert if I'm needed. Possibly you can, if necessary. But I'm a man and you're a girl, and as I see it that puts the major onus on me.'

She thought of Peter and Michael, and she couldn't see either of them sharing his views. They would think nursing woman's work and, furthermore, she felt sure they would not feel obliged to rally to the aid of an eccentric old man who chose to live on a boat in Spain instead of staying safely in England, under the wing of the welfare state.

Peter actually expressed this view the morning he saw her leaving home, and stopped the taxi to ask her where she was going. Joe had made an arrangement with a taxi driver that he should take Bianca to the clinic early every morning, return Joe to the harbour until noon and when he returned, take Bianca home until her next stint at six.

'If the old man can't afford professional help, he has no business to be out here. It's not right for a girl of your age to have to attend to the needs of some senile old fellow you hardly know'—was Peter's view of the situation.

'Rufus isn't senile,' she protested. 'Normally he's as bright as a button. I do very little for him. I'm just there for a few hours a day so that there's someone at hand if he should need attention.'

'I don't approve of it,' said Peter.

But his disapproval did not prompt him to offer his help, as he would have done had he loved her, Bianca thought afterwards.

As the days passed, and the probability that Rufus would suffer a second attack began to diminish, he went through a phase of great depression.

'I wish it had carried me off,' he said. 'I've always dreaded becoming a crock, and having to live in a home with other old people and nothing to do but watch television. Couldn't stand it. Rather be dead.'

Bianca did her best to cheer him up by pointing out that, once the hospital had discharged him, he would be able to resume his life very much as it had been before.

'For a time perhaps,' he said gloomily. 'But I shall find myself in one of those places eventually. Bound to, sooner or later.'

She discussed his low spirits with Joe the next time they had a few words together when he came on duty and she went off. Seeing him three times a day, as she did now, made it very difficult to exclude him from her thoughts. However, to do him justice, his manner towards her was more impersonal than it had been in all the time she had known him. They talked of nothing but Rufus's progress.

She wondered if Joe ever thought that Rufus's solitary old age must be his own fate if he continued to avoid the ties of marriage. But then she reflected that, not being a woman whose chances of marriage usually diminished as she grew older, at forty or even fifty Joe would still be attractive and virile; well able to find a companion for the later part of his life.

The thought of her own spinster fate cast her into a gloom almost as deep as their patient's. She knew she could never bring herself to make a second-best marriage, and although she was fortunate in having an interesting job at her fingertips, the prospect of becoming a leading genealogist was not much comfort. Tracing other people's ancestors was absorbing work, but it needed the balance of a private life peopled not by shades but by her own lively descendants.

By the time he was fit to leave the clinic, Rufus was in a more cheerful frame of mind. Joe transported him back to his boat in the car which he sometimes hired, and Bianca cooked a special homecoming lunch for the three of them.

'I can't thank you enough for all your kindness to me, my dear,' the old man said, when it was time for her to leave.

'Oh, Rufus, I've done very little. Joe has been your best help,' she answered.

'Yes, he's a fine fellow, Joe. I often wish he were my grandson. I shall leave him what little I have when I finally do depart this life,' he added, in a confidential tone.

Joe did not hear this remark as he was already on the quay while Bianca was still in the cockpit. To spare Rufus the effort of coming and going by dinghy, Joe had moved *Pago Pago* from her previous mooring to a berth alongside the quay. Berthed thus, a boat and her occupants were more exposed to the curiosity of passersby, and less secure against pilfering. But going ashore by a gangplank was a great deal quicker and easier than having to use the dinghy.

Bianca said goodbye and stepped ashore. His parting remark had reminded her of Peter's unpleasant insinuation that while her attitude to Rufus was disinterested, Joe's attentiveness might have a mercenary motive.

She felt certain there was no truth in it. Joe might have a predatory attitude to women, but she would stake her life that what he had done for Rufus had been motivated by charity in the Biblical rather than the modern sense.

For much of the way from the port to Casa Mimosa they were silent. Then suddenly, half way there, Joe said abruptly, 'Where do we go from here?'

At first she thought he was speaking literally and, since they were on a straight road and he knew the route as well as she did, the question didn't make sense to her.

'I mean do you want now to return to the way things were before Rufus's illness? Do you want us to stop seeing each other?' he asked.

'I—I think it might be best, don't you?'

'From your point of view, perhaps. Not from mine.'

Bianca said nothing, and after some moments he went on, 'I've tried not to take advantage of the situation while Rufus has been in hospital, but on my side nothing has changed. I still think we could have a lot of happiness together. Does what other people would think—if, indeed, they would give us a second thought—really matter so much to you, Bianca?'

'No, not in the sense that I care for opinion in general. Both the people whose views I most valued are dead. But I know what my parents *would* have thought, and they wouldn't have liked me to live with you.'

'Naturally not. Every generation has its own conventions, and most people find it hard to shake off the codes which prevailed when they were young. Twenty or thirty years ago it wasn't "done" for people to find out if they suited each other. Now it is.'

'Yes, but is the success rate any higher? I don't think so.'

'No, perhaps not—I won't argue on that. But the breakups, when they happen, are certainly less prolonged and painful than they used to be in the days when people rushed into marriage before they really knew each other.'

She said, 'These are reasons I've heard before, Joe. Michael used them when he was trying to persuade me to live with him, and there was a point when he almost convinced me that I should. But it would have been a mistake. I can see that now, very clearly.'

'So you would have left him,' he commented. 'Probably you would have learnt a good deal about life. Who was it who said, "We often discover what will do, by finding out what will not do"?'

'But I knew all along it would not do; that's why I said no to Michael, and why I'm still saying it, to you.'

'If at that time Michael had asked you to marry him, would you have said yes?'

'I—I don't know. Now I think not, but perhaps then ...'

'And if I were to ask you to marry me?'

Even as a hypothetical question it made her heart leap. But aloud she said quietly, '"Marriage" isn't the magic word, Joe. "Love" is, and I think we mean different things by it.'

'All right: tell me what you mean by it, and then I'll give my definition.'

'It's so hard to put into words. I know what it's not! It's not only wanting to sleep with someone.'

'Not entirely perhaps, but considerably. Particularly at the beginning,' he intervened, glancing at her. 'Is that what bothers you? The fact that when I touch you, you tremble?'

They were on a straight stretch of road, and he took his right hand off the wheel and laid it on her leg above the knee, pressing her slender thigh with his strong, square-tipped fingers.

'Don't, Joe! It isn't fair.' She used both hands to grasp his wrist and return his hand to the steering wheel.

In the light thrown back by the headlamps, she saw him grin. 'But you do,' he said, 'don't you?'

'Yes, I do. But what does that prove? I should think you could have the same effect on any number of girls. Love is more than physical attraction. It has to be mental as well. It has to be total rapport.'

'Never quite total, I fancy. There must be some differences, surely?'

'Minor ones—yes, I suppose so. But no major gulfs.'

'And you feel there are, between us?'

'Obviously. This is one of them ... what we're discussing. You want to be free and uncommitted, and I——' She broke off. One could not say to a man, especially not this one, 'I want to be loved unreservedly, passionately, for ever.'

'You can't take me on trust, or rather let me take you on that basis? You need the spurious security of a marriage contract?'

She sighed. 'No, it isn't that. I only need the security of feeling—of both parties feeling—that it will last; that however much their circumstances may change, they won't ever change in themselves.'

'A tall order, Bianca,' he said. 'The fact is that people do change. They can't help it. You won't be the same person at thirty that you are now. The whole nature of life is change.'

'Yes, physically and mentally, but not emotionally,' she countered. 'If friendship can last a lifetime, and the closest friendships often do, why shouldn't love, which is really the best kind of friendship?'

'Because friendship is rarely put to the test of continuous day-to-day contact. One has some respite from friends,' he said dryly. 'But not from a husband or wife.'

'What has made you so cynical, Joe?' she asked.

'Not cynical—merely realistic. I look at the world as it is, not as I might like it to be.'

'Well, I don't!' she answered crisply. 'I can't discard my ideals just because they don't happen to be fashionable. If what I want doesn't exist, then I'm damned if I'll settle for less. I—I'll go without love altogether. It's not the *only* thing worth living for.'

'Strong words, Bianca,' he said dryly. 'You may mean them now, but will you at thirty, I wonder?'

She didn't reply, being strung-up and close to tears. They drove the rest of the way in silence.

At the house, he switched off the engine and walked

round to open the door for her.

'Thank you for bringing me home. Goodnight, Joe ... Goodbye,' she said huskily.

He said, 'I was brought up always to see a girl safely to her front door.'

They walked up the path. At the steps rising to the veranda, Bianca said, 'I won't ask you in. I think we've said all there is to say.'

'Yes, I think we have,' he agreed. 'There's just one thing more——' He put a hand on her shoulder, and swung her to face him.

The next instant she was in his arms, being kissed with a fierce, angry passion which she had not realised had been smouldering under his unemotional manner while they were driving.

At first she struggled to free herself, but her strength was nothing compared with his. He held her imprisoned against his tall, muscular frame with as little effort as once he had carried her. Even if his embrace had been as unacceptable as Michael's, she could not have broken away from him and, just for an instant or two, the civilised, emancipated side of her resented his superior power, and his disregard for whether she wished to be kissed in this devouring fashion.

But that feeling did not last long. As he had proved to her before, the very first time he had kissed her, under the decorous surface of her nature she had a primitive alter ego who rejoiced in this despotic treatment.

As her body relaxed, his hold changed. She was no longer his startled and unwilling captive, but a compliant partner in kisses which made her feel weak and giddy. His strong hands caressed her back, gently smoothing her waist and hips, while his warm lips roved down her throat or u~ her eyelids, always returning to her mouth for a~

long, searching kiss. Even when she realised that he had pulled her blouse free of her waistband and his hands were on her bare skin, she was too deeply lulled by his kisses to recoil when the tips of his fingers played softly up and down her spine, making her tremble with longing to be in some private place, where he could possess her completely.

He held her away and looked down, his hazel eyes blazing desire but his firm mouth curiously stern.

'Something for you to remember when, in five or ten years, you're still waiting for your *beau idéal*,' he said huskily. 'I'm no knight in shining armour. Only a man looking for a woman who will take me on trust, without any safeguards or reservations. If you should change your mind, you know where to find me.'

She watched him stride down the path, get into the car and drive away. She was breathing in deep shuddering gasps, her heart and her pulses racing from the wild excitement he had roused in her. Knowing how close she had come to surrender, she was glad he had gone—and sorry that he had not stayed.

CHAPTER SEVEN

IN previous years when Bianca had come to the Casa
Mimosa in the summer for holidays, sometimes she had
seen in the distance a hill fire started, perhaps, by a carelessly discarded cigarette, or by a piece of broken bottle
which had acted as a burning-glass. More than once, lazing
in the garden with a glass of wine in her hand, she had felt
on her bare leg the sudden painful pinpoint of heat caused
by the fierce Spanish sun shining through the base of the
glass; an experience which made it easy to understand how
the tinder-dry scrub on the parched hills could start to
smoulder and then to flame. In areas thickly wooded with
pines there were signs warning people of the danger of
fire, and sometimes the municipal authorities published
notices banning the lighting of bonfires in all areas.

The fire which was to change the course of her life, and
make her see the world from a totally different perspective
than her previous view of it, began high up on a shoulder
of the mountain where she had met Joe for the second
time. At the beginning, when the breeze was blowing the
smoke upwards and fanning the flames in the direction of
the barer crags rather than downwards towards the thicker
vegetation, it seemed more than likely that the fire would
burn itself out. But when nightfall came it was still alight,
and the owners and tenants of the white villas below went
to bed uneasily aware of the scarlet glow on the mountain.
They hoped that the local people who owned and cultivated
terraces between the fire and the foreigners' properties
would know what to do to contain it.

In the early hours of the morning, she woke up and lay for some moments puzzled by an unfamiliar sound. Then she recognised it as the crackling of burning undergrowth. It sounded so close that she sprang out of bed in a panic and ran through the house, expecting to see half the mountain ablaze.

In fact the fire was not as close as it had sounded, but it covered a much larger area and clearly now there was a danger that vines and almonds as well as pines and scrub would be destroyed. Here and there she could see that old algarroba trees, from which she had seen the country people gathering the long black carob beans as fodder for mules, were shooting out clouds of sparks, their hollow trunks acting as chimneys for the flames raging round their boles.

Knowing she could not go back to sleep, she dressed and went round the house taking down her mother's paintings, and collecting one or two items of particular sentimental value in case it should become necessary temporarily to evacuate the Casa Mimosa. The villa was not insured as the structure was largely of concrete beams and cement blocks, with much less timber than an English house, and far fewer inflammable furnishings.

The air now smelt faintly acrid, and Bianca thought with a pang of all the small creatures being burned, and the acres of bare, blackened land which would be revealed when the sun rose.

Presently she went to wake up Lucy who slept with a soundness which only an earthquake would disturb.

'I'm going to see Mrs Fuller,' Bianca told her. 'She's so deaf without her hearing aid that she may not know what's going on, but she ought not to be alone in case the fire spreads that way. You'd better get up and get dressed, Lucy. I don't think we're in any danger, but other people may need help. Nothing is going to put out this fire except a really heavy downpour, and at this time of year that's a chance in a hundred.'

Mrs Fuller was the old lady on whose account she had had to refuse Joe's first invitation to sail with him. As she made her way to the rather isolated villa where Mrs Fuller had lived alone, with only her cats for company, since the death of her husband, Bianca could not help remembering the last time she had seen Joe.

She had hoped that, after three weeks, the memory of their stormy parting would have dulled a little. But it hadn't; as if it had happened the night before she could still feel the clam-like grip from which there had been no escape, and the fiercely demanding kisses which she had a despairing feeling would haunt her for ever. It was little comfort to tell herself that her affection for Michael had evaporated after a period of separation. The feelings which Joe had roused in her were like the uncontrolled blaze now raging on what the locals called the skirts of the mountain compared with the well-guarded hearth fire of her calf-love for Michael.

She found Mrs Fuller in a state of great agitation because one of the three cats was missing.

'He may have gone down to the dump—you know what a glutton he is. Come to our house with the other two, and then I'll go and look for Billy,' Bianca said reassuringly.

The cat which was missing, although well fed by his owner, had attained his enormous size by supplementing his regular diet of tinned food with titbits looted from a communal refuse bin to which, there being no house-to-house public service collection of rubbish in some rural areas, the residents had to take their garbage. Many times Bianca had seen the portly striped tom lurking behind the large bin, waiting for his next snack to arrive.

By the time Mrs Fuller, who was in her night-clothes, had dressed, and Bianca had helped her to pack some of her belongings, it was growing light. With Bianca carrying the suitcase and one cat, and the old lady cradling the other, they walked to the Casa Mimosa.

'Oh, dear, what's to become of me if my house is burned down? I have no relations, you know—no one to go to,' bewailed Mrs Fuller.

'I'm sure there's no danger of that. Bringing you to our place is just a precautionary measure,' said Bianca.

But inwardly she felt less sanguine than she tried to sound. The night had been still but most days, about mid-morning, a breeze would spring up for an hour or two, and when that happened the fire could become much worse than it already was.

Leaving her stepsister to make Mrs Fuller a cup of tea, she began to walk to the dump in the hope of finding Billy there. There was now a great pall of dark smoke rising up into the blue sky.

Before she had reached the main road, a car turned into the entrance road to the development and drew up beside her. Joe got out.

'Where are you off to?' he asked.

The sight of him made her heart leap. 'I'm going to look for a cat which is missing. What brings you here?'

'You do, of course.'

'I do?'

'If you'd heard the harbour was in flames, wouldn't you have come looking for me?'

She hesitated. 'Yes,' she admitted.

'Well then——' He gave a slight shrug. 'If you're not in need of help, I'll see if I can make myself useful elsewhere. What's this about a missing cat?'

She explained.

'A big cat, grey with dark stripes?' Joe asked.

'Yes, that's Billy. Where did you see him?'

'He's dead . . . run over at the crossroads.'

'Oh, no! Oh, poor Mrs Fuller, she'll be so upset. Was he very badly mangled?'

'No, but I've no doubt he'll be flattened before long. The Spanish are not sentimental about dead animals.'

'I know. We can't leave him there—it would distress her even more to think of him being run over again and again. If I fetch something to wrap him in, would you bring him back for me?'

'No, I draw the line at that,' he said. 'But if you have a spade, I don't mind digging a hole in that piece of woodland on the corner. Hop in'—opening the passenger door for her.

Back at the house Bianca found a spade, and Joe went to attend to the burial while she broke the news to Mrs Fuller. She was still trying to comfort the old lady when he returned.

'This is Joe Crawford,' she told her.

'How very good of you to bury my poor dear Billy,' Mrs Fuller said quaveringly.

Joe sat down beside her. 'At least he didn't suffer, Mrs Fuller. It would have been instantaneous.'

'Oh, that is a great relief. I couldn't bear to think of him lying there in pain . . . mewing for me.' Fresh tears overcame her.

Ben appeared in the doorway, and almost immediately withdrew, muttering something about dotty old ladies which made Bianca's lips tighten. She said, 'I'll get you a little brandy, Mrs Fuller.'

When she returned, Joe had placed his strong, sunburned fingers over Mrs Fuller's pale old hand, and was talking consolingly to her. But as she sipped the brandy, he rose and said he must go.

Bianca walked to the car with him and, as they crossed the veranda, she wondered if he was recalling, as she was, what had happened there the last time they had been together.

At the gate, she said, 'Thank you for coming.'

'I'll look in again later on, but for the time being I don't think this neighbourhood is likely to be much affected. From what I could see on the way here, the La Noria development is where conditions may become rather unpleasant for a time—but only unpleasant, not dangerous. This is not like California where hill fires have burned down all the timber-built houses, and people have lost their lives as well as their property.'

'But isn't there a danger of people being suffocated by the smoke?' she suggested.

'I don't think so, if they keep calm and behave sensibly.'

'What about flying sparks setting light to the beams of the verandas?'

'Not impossible, but most unlikely,' was Joe's calm reply. 'Anyone living in a house closely surrounded by pine trees will be well advised to get out of it while the fire passes, but apart from their gardens being scorched, and minor interior damage from smoke and smuts, there should be no major disasters.'

'Did you see any sign of fire engines on your way here?'

'No, but from what I heard in the restaurant last night, I believe all the *bombas* in this region are already attending a more serious outbreak of fire in a government forestry area on the inland side of that range,' he said, indicating the sierra to the west. 'From a Spanish point of view, the loss of timber is—understandably—more important than damage to foreigners' gardens.'

'Yes, of course, one sees that,' she agreed. 'All the same, I think many of the elderly residents will be very frightened if they see the flames coming towards them.'

'No doubt, but there are plenty of younger people on holiday here at the moment. They can look after the old ones, as you have with Mrs Fuller.'

'If only there isn't a wind today then I think the fire, if it does start to come in this direction, will be stopped by a wide road they've built for a new group of houses next to this one. But if the wind does get up, as it has every morning for some time now, then the sparks will blow over the road and catch the dry grass on our side. However, we must just wait and see. If you say there's no serious danger——' Bianca left this comment unfinished.

'If you're worried, I'll come back later. I can see that your stepfather isn't likely to be of much help in any kind of trouble,' he said caustically.

'No, I'm afraid he isn't,' she admitted. 'And Peter Lincoln, who would be, is away in Ibiza until tomorrow.'

'I'll come back at noon,' he told her. 'Or sooner if the wind gets up and makes the fire change its present direction. Meanwhile I'll go over to see what's happening at La Noria. See you later.'

'See you later,' she echoed.

'What a nice, kind young man,' said Mrs Fuller, when Bianca re-entered the sitting-room.

'Yes, he is,' she agreed absentmindedly.

The fact that he had promised to come back made a difference to the day which confirmed her earlier fear that she had not begun to get over him.

Shortly afterwards Lucy went to work as usual, and Ben loped off to the village, leaving Bianca alone with the old lady. Several of the nearby houses were shut up, their owners enjoying the winter climate but finding the Spanish high summer too hot for their comfort. Other houses were let to holidaymakers, most of whom seemed unconcerned by the fire. Bianca saw them driving away, bound for the beach as if nothing untoward were happening.

About eleven, they were called on by one couple who were more concerned. They were staying in La Fuente, a villa belonging to their daughter's in-laws. It was their first visit, and the wife was a nervous person who had not liked the discovery that all the windows in the house were protected by the wrought-iron grilles called *rejas*.

'They make me feel trapped,' she confided, when they had accepted Bianca's invitation to stay for coffee. 'It seems to me like being in prison. I should have preferred to have shutters had it been our house.'

'Shutters have their disadvantages, I'm told. They can warp, and they're a nuisance to close every time one goes out. With *rejas*, one can leave the windows open,' said Bianca, her eyes on the morning glory climbing round the stone arch near her seat.

The leaves had begun to flutter and, a moment later, she felt a cooling gust of air on her forehead. The breeze, which was usually so welcome but which today she had dreaded, was beginning to get up.

Midday came and passed. At one o'clock Joe had not come, but neither had the fire drawn nearer because the wind was blowing in a different direction from yesterday. It looked as if the neighbourhood of the Casa Mimosa was going to be lucky and escape the black devastation wrought by the flames in other places.

But as her anxiety on that score diminished, Bianca began to be concerned about Joe. He was not the kind of person who would promise to come back at noon, and by two o'clock still not have come, unless prevented by some very serious contingency. She began to be deeply uneasy, and by half past two her intuition was so strong that she walked round to La Fuente to ask the couple met earlier if they would mind sitting with Mrs Fuller for an hour.

'She doesn't want to go home yet, and I don't like to leave her alone. But I feel I should go and see what's happening at La Noria,' she told them.

The Greens agreed to her request, and Bianca hurried away towards the main road where she hoped to be able to hitch a lift.

Being the late Spanish lunch hour, it was not a good time of day for hitch-hiking, but she happened to be lucky and soon after setting out was being driven in the direction of La Noria.

This development, which took its name from a reconstruction of an old-fashioned well-wheel, was only a few kilometres along the road, but it looked very different from the unscathed area she had left.

The fire had passed over most of it, and people were standing about in groups, bemoaning the devastation in their gardens. Where, a few hours earlier, houses had been given privacy by thick hedges of oleander and gandula, there were now rows of charred stumps. The crab-grass lawns, planted because if necessary they would survive a summer without being watered, had the appearance of burned carpets. From snatches of conversation which she overheard as she walked about looking for the car which Joe had been driving, she gathered that the fire damage had been aggravated by the many clusters of pines left *in situ* by the developers which had acted like torches, shooting sparks in all directions and spreading the flames faster than the amateur fire-fighters had been able to beat them out.

The innermost part of the *urbanización*, beneath the steep bluffs of the mountain, was still ablaze, but as it consisted mainly of plots which had not yet been built on, the people nearer the road felt the worst of the fire was over now. It must burn itself out when it reached the foot of the rock face.

She found Joe's car parked by the supermarket, but he was nowhere to be seen.

'Have you seen the driver of that car? A very tall man ... English, but rather Spanish-looking?' she asked some people near by.

They shook their heads.

'He may be up there with the General,' one man suggested, pointing in the direction of the mountain.

'General Knight who's been organising things,' the woman beside him elaborated.

'Thank you. I'll go and see.'

It was too hot a day for hurrying. Bianca was wearing a thin cotton sun-dress, but the heat made her upper lip dewy, and a trickle of moisture ran down her back between her shoulder-blades.

The road had kerbstones, and miniature pylons to carry power lines, but the villas were scattered, and most of the land was burnt scrub. Presently she saw ahead of her a house with people and cars outside it. She began to run, hoping to see Joe among them.

He was not and, as she drew near, she was horrified to see a stretcher being carried from the house. Whoever was on it was covered by a sheet.

By the time she reached them, the stretcher-bearers had transferred their burden to the back of a station wagon.

'Please ... who is that?' Bianca panted.

'It's the old man who lived here, miss,' one of them told her.

She saw then that the shape under the cover was far shorter than Joe's long frame. 'Where is General Knight? I must speak to him.'

'That's the General over there. With the white moustache,' she was told.

She hastened towards him. 'General Knight?'

'Yes. What can I do for you?'

'I'm looking for someone ... Joe Crawford. I know he came here this morning to see if he could be useful. He's tall, about six foot one, with dark hair and hazel eyes.'

General Knight was an elderly man, but he still had a military bearing and a very sharp pair of eyes under beetling white brows.

'You're Crawford's wife?'

'No ... a friend.'

'You'd better come into the house. What is your name?' he enquired as they entered the house.

'Bianca Dawson.'

'Your friend is a plucky man, Miss Dawson,' the General told her.

'Plucky?' she queried.

'When the fire encroached on this development, most of the residents had the good sense to vacate their properties for a time and leave a small corps of men to do what they could to combat it. The risk was one of discomfort rather than danger. However, up in this area where the pines are thicker, the conflagration was more severe. Suddenly it was realised that no one had seen Mr Knight, the owner of this villa. He was known to be a sick man, on whom any agitation might have a critical effect. He was also rather unpopular, hence the lack of concern for his welfare. The villa was almost cut off when Crawford went to his aid. He got through by the skin of his teeth. Then the blaze closed in and no more was seen of either of them until the fire had passed on. Knight was found to be dead. According to a doctor who's staying here, he had been dead for some time, probably since yesterday.'

'And Joe?' she asked, in a taut voice.

'He's missing. We assume that, having found Knight beyond aid, he attempted to get back through the fire. It may be that he has succeeded. If not, I'm afraid he's trapped.'

'Trapped?' she whispered. In spite of the heat of the day, her blood seemed to freeze.

'Up there'—he made a gesture towards the mountain— 'in what is known as a *barranco*—a steep gully,' he added explanatorily, in case she did not know the Spanish word. 'The fire is burning all round the mouth of the *barranco*. Crawford's only way out is to climb up the cliffs to the plateau and make his way down by a mule-track.'

'But they're almost sheer, and ... and'—her voice shook —'I was told that pink rock is dangerous.'

'I don't know,' the General answered. 'And I don't know Crawford as well as you do. But obviously he's an extremely fit man, and not easily daunted, I should say. He'll get out if anyone can.'

If anyone can. The words had a knell-like ring.

Bianca hurried outside and shaded her eyes against the glare to scan the rocks rising up from the back of the gully. When the General joined her, she said, 'If he were climbing we'd see him.'

'Not necessarily. The cliffs have a number of large crevices in them. What climbers call "chimneys", I believe. He may be inside one of those, and it's also possible that he won't attempt to reach the top but will merely stay out of reach of the flames until they've subsided. Then he'll come down the way he went up. We shouldn't think the worst at this stage.'

She averted her face to hide the tears in her eyes, the sudden trembling of her lips. She knew then that, if Joe was dead, the rest of her life would be an interminable void.

She would never meet another man like him. Always, until she was old, she would be sick with regret that, having known him, having recognised all his fine qualities, she had lacked the courage to grasp the happiness he had offered her.

What did marriage matter, or permanence? What did anything matter but to fill one's life with all the riches which came one's way; love, laughter, beauty, excitement —but first, and best of all, love.

Oh, fool! Stupid fool! she thought, with bitter self-reproach. She could see now, with painful clarity, that she had held back from taking what Joe had to offer not by a principle but by a price.

The price of her love had been marriage, and girls who gave love for less she had thought unwise and misguided. But had she ever thought it *wrong* to live with a man, provided that he was free, and no child resulted? No, she had not. More than half the world's greatest love affairs had never been approved by Church or State, yet who condemned the participants? They were remembered with envy for letting love sweep them away.

Now that it might be too late, she saw how niggardly her previous attitude had been. Not 'loving and giving' as a Friday's child was supposed to be, but careful and cowardly.

'Are you on holiday here?' the General asked her.

With an effort, she mastered her emotion. 'No, we live here. Joe has a boat in the harbour. He plays the piano at El Delfin. Have you never been there?'

'No, my wife and I don't often patronise the local restaurants. We prefer home cooking,' he said. 'Plays the piano, eh? You surprise me. Should have put him down as a military man like myself. I suppose that's because of his bearing. Holds himself well; unusual in a young man nowadays unless he's had some Service training.'

'He spent some time in the Spanish Foreign Legion,' she explained.

'Did he, by Jove? Enterprising! Now look here, Miss Dawson, the best thing you can do is to come along to my house and stay with my wife while I send a couple of chaps up there to see if there's any sign of him.'

'I'd rather go with them.'

'No, no, that won't do at all. You can't go tramping about on burnt land. Ruin your sandals and get yourself filthy to no purpose. Much better to stay with my wife,' he said, on a note of command.

Bianca closed her mind to the thought of what the men might find at the head of the *barranco* if, strong and agile as he was, Joe had not been able to climb out of reach of the fire. She must not lose hope. Not yet.

His wife, when the General had briskly explained the position, received Bianca into her home with the understanding manner of a woman who knows from experience the cruel anxiety of waiting for news of a man who may not come back.

'Perhaps you wouldn't mind helping me to deal with some of this dirt which has filtered through the windows,' she said, after her husband had left the house.

She gave Bianca a cloth and suggested she should wipe over the marble worktops in the kitchen, while she herself vacuumed up smuts in the adjoining dining area.

The task was what Bianca needed to help her to keep control of herself. Only once, as she rinsed out the cloth at the sink, did she glance out of the window. The Knights' garden marched with an unsold site where, not long ago, the outcrops of rock must have been interspersed with bushes of gorse and wild rosemary. The sight of it now, blackened and ugly, made her avoid a second look.

Please don't let him be dead! she prayed silently. She was not religious; it was just a deep-seated instinct to beg to be spared the anguish of never seeing him again, of knowing he had died in pain, with most of his life still ahead of him.

I can't bear it, she thought. How can I go on living without him? I didn't know how much I loved him.

A car drew up outside the house. She let the cloth fall and hurried to see who it was, closely followed by Mrs Knight.

To her surprise she saw Mr Green getting out of the driver's seat, followed by General Knight who had been in the rear. A moment later a tall, charcoal-blackened figure emerged from the offside front seat where because of the angle of view from the Knights' first floor *naya*, he had not been immediately visible.

'*Joe!*' She flew down the curved flight of stairs to ground level and would have flung herself at him had the General not restrained her.

'Careful, Miss Dawson! He's not only as black as pitch, but he's burnt his arm.'

She saw then that Joe's left arm was wrapped in what looked like a clean pillow-case.

'Oh, Joe ... you're safe!' she exclaimed hoarsely.

He said quietly, 'Yes, I'm fine. I'm sorry I didn't turn up when I said I would. I thought you might be concerned, which is why I went straight to your house, only to find you'd come down here, looking for me.'

He looked like a miner straight from the coal-face; his clothes grimed, his face filmed with soot and streaked with sweat, his hair matt instead of glossy.

'Come inside and let me look at that arm,' said Mrs Knight. 'I'm a nurse—or rather I was.' She smiled at Bianca, sharing her relief and happiness. 'That's how I met my husband. I was nursing in India, and he'd been wounded in Burma.'

The removal of the pillow-case revealed a long, narrow burn on Joe's forearm which made Bianca flinch. But the older woman said calmly, 'The sooner this is treated the better. Then we'll wrap it in plastic, and you can clean up under the shower and borrow some of my husband's clothes before going to see a doctor and get the shots you should have.'

'You gave us some bad moments, Crawford. What happened?' enquired the General.

Joe said, 'As you must know by now, I found the old man already dead. Rather than hang about in the house until the fire had passed round it, I decided to go up the gully and get out that way. But, as I've told you, when I arrived at Bianca's house she had gone, and Mr Green very kindly offered me a lift.'

'Rather risky to assume you could get out by way of the gully, wasn't it?' was the General's comment.

'Not really, sir. I've explored this terrain fairly thoroughly, and it's not as tricky as it looks.' He glanced at what Mrs Knight was doing to his arm. By now he was seated on a chair in the kitchen, with the rest of them grouped round him. 'I've had some training in climbing,' he added casually.

Mr Green said, 'I think I'd better be getting back to my wife and the old lady. What about you, Miss Dawson? Shall I run you back with me?'

She looked at Joe. Had they been alone, she would have been explicit. With three people looking on, she chose a more oblique way to tell him how much his safety meant to her. 'If your arm is out of action, perhaps you'd like me to cook your supper for you?'

'Thanks, Bianca, but that isn't necessary. I shall go to the restaurant as usual.'

'But surely you won't work tonight? How can you play with your arm in a sling?' she objected.

'Good God! A sling isn't necessary. I don't say my playing will be improved, but it's only background music, you know, and at this time of year when the place is crowded no one will notice a few more wrong notes than usual.'

'No, it's only a superficial burn,' put in Mrs Knight. 'It looks rather nasty at the moment, but it shouldn't take long to heal.'

Bianca was aware that Mr Green was twiddling his keys in the manner of someone trying not to show impatience but keen to be on their way.

She said, 'Well ... I'm more than thankful you're all right.'

In spite of their audience, she was on the point of dropping a light but she hoped, to him, significant kiss on his dirt-smeared cheek when he checked her impulse by saying carelessly, 'You needn't have worried—I was never in the slightest danger. Anyway, you can forget the fire in your area now. It's burned itself out in that direction and although it's still alight elsewhere, it can't turn back over burnt ground.'

'That's good news. My wife will be relieved. What with long delays at both airports because of go-slows, and then her worry about the fire, our holiday has got off to a rather bad start,' said Mr Green. 'Not at all ... don't mention it' —this in response to Joe's thanks for the lift and apology for dirtying his car.

'Goodbye, Joe,' said Bianca.

After what she had been through, emotionally, in the past forty minutes, to have to say goodbye and leave him with the Knights was an anticlimax. But what else could she do? One could not say baldly, in public, 'I've changed my mind. I will come and live with you.'

With his usual good manners, he rose from the chair to say, 'Goodbye, Bianca.'

What he was thinking, she could not tell. Perhaps there was nothing in his mind but the discomfort from his burnt arm and the wish for a shower. Possibly he had no inkling that she too was not unscathed. The fire had not harmed her physically, but it had scarred her spirit. She would never be able to forget the terror of fearing him lost to her.

'A rather fine-looking young man, I should think, when he's clean,' remarked Mr Green, as they drove away from the Knights' villa.

'Yes, he is,' she agreed, with a small pang of pleasure at hearing Joe praised.

She wished now she had been much less British, much less stiff-upper-lipped. A Spanish girl, distraught with anxiety, would not have attempted to hide her misery. If Bianca had allowed herself to cry while waiting for news of him, Joe would have seen for himself what she had been through. Or even if she had told Mrs Knight how desperate she felt, the General's wife might now be saying, 'Poor Miss Dawson was terribly worried about you.' Not that Joe didn't already know that she cared for him. He did. The only thing he did not know was that now she was his without reserve.

CHAPTER EIGHT

HAD she been a completely free agent, the following morning Bianca would have acted on her decision to throw in her lot with Joe by going to the harbour and making her changed outlook clear to him.

What held her back now was the feeling that such an action on her part must set a bad example to Lucy. Example rather than precept had been the foundation of her own upbringing, and that concept was now so deeply ingrained in her character that she could not dismiss the possible effect of her action on her young stepsister as something which need not trouble her.

If she, long regarded by Lucy as a pattern of old-fashioned morality, threw her bonnet over the windmill, it must at once undermine all her own and her mother's influence on the girl; an influence which, lately, she had felt to be a good deal more effective than had been apparent during Lucy's unruly phase.

It was one thing for someone such as herself, grown-up and level-headed, to live with the man she loved. But if her still immature stepsister were to follow suit, it could be the first step on the road to a series of ill-judged relationships leading perhaps, at the end, to the degradation and unhappiness of becoming wholly promiscuous. Bianca knew it would lie very heavily on her conscience if she felt even partially responsible for steering Lucy towards that end.

However, while she was wrestling with this fresh set of scruples, the matter was settled for her by Lucy running off to England. The first Bianca knew of it was when, on the second day after the fire, she returned from marketing to find a note on the kitchen table.

Dear B, Lucy had written.

By the time you read this I shall be on the coach to England. Don't worry about me. As soon as I get there, I shall telephone Mark and he'll look after me. I couldn't tell you beforehand because I know you would have tried to stop me, and I can't see the point of wasting any more time. See you some time. Good luck. Lucy.

Bianca read the note twice, her reaction a mixture of concern and relief. It would have been hypocrisy to pretend that she was not glad to be rid of Lucy. But was it her duty to go after her? Or should she accept the *fait accompli* and, with it, the freedom to follow her own inclinations?

When Ben came in, some time later, she broke the news to him, expecting him to receive it with surprise followed by indifference. Had she realised that he had been celebrating the sale of several pictures to tourists who had bought one displayed in the village bar and come to the house to buy others, she would have delayed telling him until the morning. But with Ben it was often difficult to tell whether he was only lightly pickled or had been imbibing heavily. Preoccupied with the major change which was about to take place in her own life, Bianca was taken aback when Ben's reaction, far from being apathetic, was a melodramatic enactment of a Victorian father's response to his daughter's abduction.

'What! You've let her run off to the son of that puffed-up fool down the road. Can't stand the bloke—never could. Thinks because he's got money he can ride rough-shod

over everybody. Where's Lucy's letter to me?' he demanded
irately.

'In your room, I expect. I haven't looked.' Bianca's heart
sank as she realised her stepfather's condition.

Her guess was correct. Lucy had left an equally brief
note for him in his bedroom. Had he had a few brandies
more, Ben might have shed some maudlin tears and retired
to sleep off his sorrows. Instead he took it into his head
that Peter must drive to the border, intercept the coach
and bring Lucy back.

'Ben, you're being absurd. He can't do that. It's not his
place to interfere. Lucy is your responsibility, but even if
you had a car and were fit to drive it, you couldn't drag her
back against her will,' she said, with unwonted acerbity.

She had borne with Ben for a long time, and was reaching the end of her tether with him.

'Maybe I can't, but he can. It's his son who's inveigled
her into this, so it's up to Lincoln to stop her. Don't tell me
that damned great car he drives can't catch up the coach.
Course it can—easily. I'll go and tell him. Either my little
girl is brought back here in twenty-four hours, or I'll lay a
complaint to the Guardia, and Lincoln will find himself de-
ported. Serve him right ... telling Juanita she ought not to
serve me. Never heard such cheek!'

From these last remarks, Bianca realised that it was not
concern about Lucy which was at the root of Ben's hostile
attitude to Peter.

All the way between the two houses, she attempted to
reason with her stepfather. But neither argument nor
physical restraint could divert him from his determination
to have a showdown with Peter. He shook off her clutch on
his arm, and refused to listen to her.

She had hoped Peter might be out, but unfortunately he
was at home. He listened in silence to Ben's tirade, while

Bianca stood by, wondering what he would say when the other man finally drew breath. She was beyond feeling embarrassment.

To her surprise, when Ben finished ranting, Peter said, 'Certainly the girl must be fetched back. But I don't propose to chase after the coach. It takes thirty-six hours to reach London. I'll run you to the airport tomorrow morning, and you can be there to meet her when she arrives. You've had a shock, Hollis. Better have a drink to pull you together.' He went to his drinks cupboard and poured out a triple brandy.

Any man with a vestige of self-respect left would have dashed the glass from his hand, but Ben took it and gulped half the contents. Then he flopped into the nearest chair, and Bianca realised that Peter had handled the situation in the best possible way. The liquor which had induced Ben's wrath had also douched it. All at once his eyes had the glazed look which meant that in ten minutes or less he would be insensible.

'I'll get Tomás to give me a hand to take him back to your house,' said Peter, referring to the Spaniard who since Sheila's death had helped him to keep the garden in order. 'I don't want him lying there all night'—with a contemptuous glance at the now drowsy Ben.

Later, when Ben had been deposited on his bed and the gardener had gone back to his work, Peter told her, 'I meant what I said. He's going to be on that plane tomorrow, and I shall be with him to see that he does meet the coach. If it's true—which it may not be—that Mark has encouraged Lucy to go to him, and if he intends to marry her, then I suppose I can't stop him. Although I don't mind telling you, Bianca, I shall try. But if I can't make him see sense, then I'm not going to have him encumbered as you and your mother have been encumbered. Hollis is going to be treated, whether he likes it or not.'

She said uncertainly, 'As long as you're doing it for Mark's sake, and not for mine, Peter?'

'No, no—I've accepted now that what I had hoped can never be. Perhaps you were right. Perhaps the age difference between us is too great,' he conceded. 'My advice to you now is to put this place on the market while you have the chance. This is a good time to sell and, if you make the price reasonable, you could have it off your hands in a matter of weeks. Then you can't be lumbered with him again. Blood may be thicker than water, but the fact that your mother made a mistake in her second marriage doesn't mean that you have to pay for it indefinitely, my dear. Remake your life while you can. Sell up, go back to England, and forget all the troubles you've had here.'

'Ben hasn't gone with you yet. He may refuse,' she said, sighing.

But it seemed that Peter had more steel in him than she had realised, and the following day he bullied Ben into going with him although, as she had foreseen, this was not achieved without some conflict of wills. But just as yesterday she had been no match for Ben's intoxicated obstinacy, he in the throes of a hangover was no match for Peter's determination.

When they had driven away, Bianca could hardly believe that, at least for a time, she was free to go her own way—which really meant free to go to Joe.

But she could not go to him immediately because Peter had arranged to ring her up at his house that evening, and after that Joe would be working. She would have to wait until tomorrow, which would really be better because it would give her time to unwind; a breathing space between the past and the future.

How long a future? an inner voice seemed to murmur.

But Bianca ignored it and lay in the sun thinking that, this time tomorrow, she might be lying in Joe's arms, and tomorrow was as far ahead as she wanted to look.

The instant she awoke the next morning, she knew it was a very special day—in effect her wedding day.

She ate her breakfast in the garden, listening to the lovely slow second movement of Joaquin Rodrigo's Concierto de Aranjuez. The notes of the soloist's guitar seemed to float into the golden air like bright bubbles of sound. Her mother had called it 'the essence of Spain' and had played it often. Bianca thought it likely that this was the last time she would listen to it in this setting as she meant to take Peter's advice and put the Casa Mimosa up for sale.

His telephone call the previous evening had been brief. He and Ben had been waiting for Lucy when she arrived at the coach station, and were on the point of setting out to see his son. He would keep Bianca informed.

Now, leisurely eating the pale apricot flesh of the melon which was her breakfast, she felt she would not much mind if he failed to keep in touch. She wanted, at least for a time, to concentrate exclusively on her own life; to ignore the rest of the world.

It was no use going to the harbour too early, so she spent some time in the town looking in the windows of the estate agencies to gain some idea of what the house might fetch. She thought she might buy a small flat. A long time ago she had read in a magazine an article which had dealt with the practical side of women's new freedom to live with their lovers openly without being shunned by the more conventional members of society.

'Never give up your place and move into his place,' the writer of the article had advised; her reason being that, if the relationship foundered, the man would still have a roof but the girl would find herself homeless. She had, Bianca remembered, taken the point even further, recommending that from the outset it should be agreed that the couple would live partly in the man's home and partly in the woman's.

Somehow Bianca could not see Joe agreeing to an arrangement of that nature. She felt sure he would expect her to live on *La Libertad*. But there was no reason why she should not have a flat, even if they never used it. It would be somewhere to keep things which had belonged to her parents and with which she did not want to part; and, if let to holidaymakers during the summer, it could provide her with a small income.

However, these down-to-earth thoughts were far from her mind as she made her way to the harbour.

Joe was not on deck, but he appeared within seconds of her hail. His eyebrows lifted in surprise. '*Buenas, señorita!*' he said, somewhat sardonically.

'*Buenas!* May I come aboard?'

'With pleasure.'

He came to fetch her, handing her into the dinghy with his usual firm clasp. His left arm, she noticed, had only a light dressing over the burn.

'How is your arm?' she asked. 'I suppose you can't swim until it's better?'

'It would take more than this to keep me out of the sea in this heat. But I keep it covered at other times.'

By now she had become as nimble at climbing inboard as if she had been doing it all her life instead of only this summer.

'What can I do for you, Bianca?' he asked, as he joined her in the cockpit.

'C-could we go below? It's a ... a rather private matter.'

'Why not? If you're sure your pristine reputation will survive being seen going below with me,' he added, with an edge of sarcasm.

Out of sight and earshot of the people berthed alongside, she said, 'My reputation is no longer so important to me. I—I've changed my mind, Joe. If ... if you still want me, here I am.'

For some moment he did not react. They looked at each other; her cheeks slightly flushed, her eyes shy. Joe's expression had never been more unreadable. She felt a flicker of panic in case he had changed *his* mind.

Then he took her face between his hands, and she saw a warm smile light his eyes before he said huskily, 'I want you,' and kissed her softly on the mouth.

Some time later he let her go and moved away to close the hatch. Then he came back and held out his hand, and she knew he was about to lead her through to his cabin in the bows. Without hesitation she slipped her hand into his.

But outside his private quarters, which she had never seen before, Joe uttered a sound which was part exclamation, part groan.

'Goddammit! I'd forgotten the Maxwells.'

'Who are they?' she queried.

'Some people I met at the beach and invited to come for a sail today. They're due here at half-past eleven, and it's now'—glancing at his watch—'twenty-four minutes past.' A rueful grin tugged at his mouth. 'I can't very well tell them the trip is off because my girl has turned up unexpectedly, and I'd much rather take her to bed. I'm sorry, my dear. I'm afraid there's nothing else for it but to take these people for a quick flip round the bay, and get rid of them as soon as we decently can.'

'It doesn't matter. There's all tonight. It is your night off as usual, isn't it?'

'It is, but even if it weren't, I should take it.' He unfastened the hatch and they stepped up into the sunshine. 'Here they come now,' he said, looking along the quay to where a man and a woman were walking briskly in their direction, carrying between them a cool bag. 'I'll go to meet them.' He slipped his arm round her and held her close to his side for a moment. 'You're sure you won't have had second thoughts by the time we're on our own again? If I felt there was any danger of that, I'd tell them to go to the devil.'

'No, I'm here to stay this time, for as long as we're happy together,' she promised.

She hoped he might say something like 'That could be for ever,' but he didn't. He only dropped a swift kiss on the top of her head, and went to meet his unwelcome guests.

The Maxwells proved to be a couple whose company, on any other day, Bianca would have enjoyed, and indeed did enjoy as things were. Steve Maxwell was a geologist whose work had taken him all over the world. He and Mary had come to Spain because, although still in their forties, they felt the need of a base to which, eventually, they could retire. Several years spent in South America had given them a good command of Spanish, and made Spain top of their list of suitable countries.

Having married very young, they had two grown-up children, but Mary referred to them less than women of her age were prone to do. It was plain that to her the world revolved around her husband. She had had to give up her own career to accompany him on his travels, but had obviously found the time spent in other countries a more than adequate compensation for the waste of her training as a lawyer.

'My father was a country town solicitor who, having no

sons, encouraged me to follow in his footsteps,' she explained to Bianca. 'I was actually engaged to one of Dad's junior partners when I met Steve. It took a good deal of courage to upset my parents, and my fiancé and his parents, by breaking off the engagement. But I knew the first time I met Steve that he was the only man for me.'

'Where are your children?' asked Bianca.

They were all in the cockpit, drinking some of the *espumoso* wine which the Maxwells had brought in the cool bag as their contribution to the outing, but the two men were having a separate conversation.

'My son is studying medicine, and my daughter is a ballet dancer with a burning desire to become a prima ballerina. But I rather suspect that before she achieves that ambition, some young man will sweep her off her feet, as Steve did me,' said Mary Maxwell. 'But enough of my family. Tell me about yourself. Are you on holiday here?'

Bianca explained the circumstances which had brought her to Spain. She felt that the older woman must be curious about her connection with Joe, but Mrs Maxwell did not probe.

Having sailed to a quiet cove, Joe suggested a bathe before lunch. The Maxwells, who were both good swimmers, struck out for the beach, but Joe and Bianca did not join them.

Coming close to her and treading water, he said, 'What changed your mind?'

'The fire ... thinking that you were dead.'

'What are your family going to think when you don't go home tonight?'

'They aren't there.' She explained what had happened.

'You do realise that life with me won't be a luxury cruise? In fact we might sometimes be reduced to really short commons.'

'I'm not accustomed to luxury. Who needs it?' she answered cheerfully.

'Most girls want more than I can offer.'

'You're lucky you came across me, then.' She was determined to keep a very light touch. 'The Maxwells are nice people, aren't they?'

'I thought so the first time I met them. I could do without them today.' Suddenly he duck-dived under the water and, after an interval, she felt a light clasp on her ankle and drew in a deep breath of air before she was drawn under the surface.

She had never been kissed underwater before. It was a curious sensation to be clasped in Joe's strong brown arms in that alien world beneath the sea. She guessed that his lung capacity was considerably greater than hers, and that he could stay down much longer. But she felt no alarm that he might keep her under for too long. Her confidence in him was total. Even drowning, she thought, would not be a fearful end as long as he held her close.

They came up a yard apart, and no one watching from the beach could have known what had happened below the glinting surface of the water. Joe raked dark wet hair off his forehead, and grinned at her, tanned and glistening.

'A foretaste of pleasures in store when we can get rid of our guests.'

His eyes held a leonine gleam which sent a small shudder through her.

They had lunch in the shade of the awning and, after a suitable interval, the two men went snorkeling by the rocks at the foot of the cliffs.

'He's great fun, your Joe,' said Mrs Maxwell, as Bianca topped up their glasses with the last of the wine they had drunk with lunch.

' "My" Joe?' Bianca said questioningly.

'I felt you were more than just sailing companions. Perhaps I was wrong.'

'No, you were right, but how did you guess?'

As far as Bianca could recall, they had not in the presence of the Maxwells, exchanged any touch or glance which would have made plain that they were, or soon would be, lovers.

'I'm not sure. You just seem to match,' said Mrs Maxwell.

'Do we? I hope so.'

Suddenly Bianca could not help envying her the slim band of platinum she wore on her left hand. She had known since the day of the fire that to love and be loved was the only essential of happiness: nothing else really mattered. But it would have been heaven to have the pledge of Joe's love on her finger. Wholly committed as she was to him, she could not but be conscious that what he had said to her earlier, 'I want you', was not the same as 'I love you.'

Steve Maxwell was a competent helmsman and on the way back to harbour Joe left him in charge of the wheel, and came forward to sit with Bianca on the coach roof.

'I said earlier that the budget might sometimes be tight, but it isn't at present. Would you like to dine out in style tonight?'

He mentioned the two most expensive restaurants in the area, at one of which she had seen him with the beautiful and wealthy older woman whose relationship with him had troubled her for a time. Since then she had put Mrs Russell out of her mind, and this unexpected reminder of her jarred slightly.

She said, 'I don't think there's much chance of getting a table without a reservation. But anyway I'd just as soon dine on board, wouldn't you?'

'I would—yes. But I don't want you to feel disappointed.

At any other time of year we could take off to one of the islands for a week or two, but I think Piet would feel rather aggrieved if I stopped working for him without at least some advance warning.'

'Oh, no, you couldn't do that. It wouldn't be right,' she agreed. 'And we shall be together all day.'

'And much of the night.' He put his arm round her and kissed the end of her eyebrow. 'Not long now before we're alone. Did you remember to bring your toothbrush? If not, I've some spares on board.'

'Yes, that's practically all I did pack. My nightie, slippers and toothbrush.'

'You could have left out the nightie,' he said, with a look which made her blush slightly, and made him smile at the sudden pinkness underlying her sun-tan. The arm round her tightened a little. His fingers caressed her bare arm. 'Am I the first, Bianca?'

'Yes ... yes. Didn't you know?'

'I thought it possible, but there was that chap Michael Leigh, and you are over twenty-one.'

'Is it so rare for someone of my age not to have had any lovers?'

'They say so, but who really knows? I should think statistics on sex are even less reliable than most statistics.'

She wanted to answer 'I don't think of it as sex, but as love'. But love was a word she was going to be careful not to use until—if ever—he used it.

She turned her cheek against his shoulder and saw, close to her face, the strong brown column of his neck and the square, forceful jut of his chin, the skin now darkened by the beard which she knew he shaved before going to play at El Delfin. She lifted her hand to touch the line of his jaw, finding the texture of his skin as exciting as the rest of his masculinity—the shoulders which were so much broader than her own, the bicipital muscles which swelled under the flesh of his upper arm even when he was not exerting his strength, and the lean hips and long, long legs which made him look down not only at her but at most of his own sex.

Joe turned his head to kiss her exploring fingers. 'When we've berthed I must shave, or tomorrow you'll have a sore face, *vida mia*.'

Bianca wondered if he used a Spanish endearment because it was somehow more non-committal than an English one. Perhaps his first girl had been Spanish although, from what she had heard, at the time he had been serving Spain the girls of the country had still led much more sedate lives than their counterparts in the more permissive countries of northern Europe.

It seemed unlikely that a young *legionario* would have had any opportunity to sow his wild oats with a Spanish girl of respectable family. There must have been many girls since then. How many she did not care, as long as she was the last. But, inexperienced as she was, could she hope to hold him?

Joe took over the helm before they berthed. In their absence, another craft had taken his usual mooring, but he only shrugged and expertly slid *La Libertad* into a berth between a yacht registered in Miami and one of the several piers which jutted out from the main quay. When *La Libertad* had been made fast, the Maxwells had a final drink before taking their leave.

'It's been a marvellous day. We've both thoroughly enjoyed ourselves. We wondered if you and Bianca would care to lunch with us at what's said to be an excellent fish restaurant about twenty miles south?' said Steve Maxwell, as they were leaving.

'We'd be delighted,' said Joe. 'But we're rather tied up

all this week. Could we make it some time next week?'

A date was agreed, and the older couple stepped ashore. Then Joe was hailed by another boat-owner and Bianca went below to start washing up the lunch things which were stacked in the sink.

She had scarcely begun before he was back. She heard him close and bolt the hatchway. In a sudden flurry of shyness and uncertainty, she called out, 'Would you like a cup of tea?'

He came into view, smiling at her, his hazel eyes at their most quizzical, one dark eyebrow cocked. 'Are you serious? There's only one thing I want—you, my lovely. Dry your hands and come here.'

She did as he told her, her heart beginning to thud against her ribs.

'Are you nervous? There's no need to be.' He drew her against him and began to kiss her, softly at first and then, as she relaxed, less gently. After a while she became aware that he was steering her backwards towards his cabin in the bows. She kept her eyes closed, and let him lead her where he wished.

When she felt his fingers unfastening the buttons of the shirt she had put on to sail back to harbour, she trembled but submitted willingly as, keeping his mouth on hers, he took her arms from his shoulders and removed the shirt altogether. Briefly, his hands clasped the soft inward curve of her waist before sliding up over her back to unhook the clip of her bikini with one hand and untie the halter with the other. The skimpy top was cast aside and she was left in only her white linen shorts.

It was at this moment that a thunderous banging somewhere aft made Joe lift his head and Bianca open her eyes.

'What is it?' she whispered bewilderedly.

'Someone pounding on the hatch. What in hell's name

does the fool want?' he exclaimed, in a voice rough with passion.

The loud knocking continued, and now they could hear an urgent voice calling to Joe in rapid Spanish.

'I shall have to see who it is.' With one easy movement he swept her up in his arms and carried her to the bunk. There he laid her down and, for a moment, bent to press a hot kiss on one of the triangles of paler skin which was never or rarely exposed to the sun.

'I shan't be long.'

For some seconds after he left her, Bianca lay breathless and quivering, his final kiss burning the flesh over her wildly beating heart.

Then, hearing him unbolt the hatch, she knew in a flash that only something of great importance could make someone hammer the wood so violently.

Dazed by the storm of sensations through which she had passed, she staggered to her feet and, retrieving her shirt, put it on. Her fingers shook as she struggled to fasten the buttons. She could still feel Joe's kisses on her mouth, and a strange, thrilling ache lingered in the pit of her stomach. He had made her feel wild and wanton, and more fully alive than ever before.

She followed him through to the cockpit where a young Spaniard, who seemed vaguely familiar, was talking too fast for her to follow him.

Joe checked the flow with a gesture, and turned to Bianca. 'This is one of the waiters from El Delfin. They've had an extremely urgent call for me, I must ring back at once.'

'Shall I come with you?' she asked.

'No, I'm going on the back of his motor-bike. I'll be back very soon.' A hand on her shoulder, he kissed her lightly on the lips.

Then he and the Spaniard sprang ashore, and seconds later they were roaring away on the waiter's motor-cycle.

By the time the throb of the engine had died away in the distance, Bianca too had stepped ashore. Slowly she climbed the steps to the top of the harbour wall from which vantage point she could watch them circling the fishing boat harbour and following the coast road until they turned off and were lost to view.

She found she was shivering slightly and, crossing her arms over her chest, she gave her upper arms a brisk friction rub as if it were physical cold which was causing her tremors. But though cooler by the sea than inland, the early evening was as balmy as usual, and she knew it was a nervous reaction.

The fact that she could not begin to guess who had rung Joe, or for what reason, was an unwelcome reminder of how little she knew about the man with whom, but for this interruption, she would be sharing one of the most crucial and unforgettable experiences of her life.

About half an hour later there was still no sign of the motor-cycle coming back. Suddenly she was startled to recognise the Dutchman who owned El Delfin walking briskly along the quay towards *La Libertad*. He must have come in a car, and left it beyond the barrier. She flew down the steps to intercept him.

'Where's Joe?' she asked, as they came abreast.

'Ah, Miss Dawson—Good evening. Joe is on his way to the airport. With luck, he may just make the last flight.'

'The last flight?' she echoed bewilderedly.

'Yes, but if he does catch the plane, it will be with only minutes to spare. There was no time to come back here and pack a bag, or say goodbye. He asked me to give you this.'

The Dutchman took from his pocket a slip of paper

torn from a telephone note-pad and folded to cover the writing on it.

The message was not very explanatory. *Sorry, must leave at once. Will ring you noon tomorrow to explain. J.*— was all Joe had written.

The omission of the word Love before his initial struck her like a blow. People added Love to the most trivial messages. In the context of a hastily scribbled note such as this, its absence seemed more significant than its presence would have done.

'He says he'll telephone tomorrow. I suppose he must mean to your number.'

The Dutchman nodded. 'Undoubtedly.'

'But he doesn't say why he had to leave in such a hurry. Did he tell you what had happened?'

He shook his head. 'There wasn't time. As soon as he had finished speaking to the Marbella number, he called the airport to find out what time the next flight left. While he was making the call, he asked me if I would lend him the cash for the fare, and he noticed a taxi bringing some customers to the restaurant and asked one of my waiters to hold it for him. By the time I had fetched the necessary amount of money from my safe, he was ready to leave. Fortunately his passport was also in the safe, or he would have lost time coming back to the boat for it. He prefers to keep his papers and valuables ashore if he can arrange it.'

'I see,' she said dully. 'In that case we shall have to wait until tomorrow to find out what's happened.'

'Unless he misses the plane and rings up tonight, from the airport or an hotel. Would you like to come back to the restaurant with me in case that should happen?'

She shook her head. 'Thank you, it's kind of you to suggest it, but I expect he'll catch the plane. I'll lock up the boat and go home. I'll see you tomorrow. Goodnight.'

'Goodnight,' he replied.

As they turned away from each other, something clicked in Bianca's memory. 'The Marbella number,' he had said. The last time she had heard Marbella mentioned had been after Joe introduced her to Mrs Russell. It was she, the rich widow, who had referred to the Andalucian resort, saying she felt it might suit her better than the quieter, less sophisticated Costa Blanca.

Bianca turned to the Dutchman again. 'You said the call came from Marbella. Do you happen to know the caller's name? Was it a Mrs Russell?'

He nodded. 'That's so—Mrs Helen Russell. Do you know her?'

'We've met. She spent a few days here some weeks ago. Goodnight.'

For the second time she turned away, and walked slowly back to *La Libertad*.

'An extremely urgent call', Joe had said, when first he had received the message.

But was it really? Or was it merely the caprice of a woman rich enough to indulge her every whim; the whim of the moment being to summon to her side, without notice, and from hundreds of miles away, a man who suited her mood better than any of those more readily available.

I don't believe it ... I *won't* believe it, thought Bianca. Joe wouldn't go ... he wouldn't drop me for her. Not tonight. He couldn't!

Couldn't he? queried a cynical demon in her mind. Why not? What stronger claim do you have on him. You're younger than she is, but not as beautiful, and no more bedworthy. Why should he mind passing up the chance to make love to you if, by midnight, he will have her in his arms?

CHAPTER NINE

ALTHOUGH it had been her intention, upon parting from the Dutchman, to lock up *La Libertad* and go back to the Casa Mimosa, by the time she had made the boat tidy Bianca had changed her mind and decided to spend the night on board.

Having restored the galley to its customary state of immaculate tidiness, she returned to Joe's cabin where, before, she had been in no state to notice her surroundings.

There was, as she had expected there might me, a good deal more evidence of the character of the boat's owner in the compact but comfortable cabin than elsewhere on board. The first things to catch her eye were two photographs, their frames screwed to the bulkhead above a Formica counter which spanned two banks of drawers and appeared to double as a dressing table and writing desk.

One of the photographs was of an elderly woman who, a moment before the picture was taken, had been weeding a herbaceous border but was snapped sitting back on her heels, her trowel momentarily at rest while she smiled towards the camera. Was this the grandmother who had given Joe his first piano lessons? wondered Bianca. If so, she looked a darling; not in the cosy, cottage-loaf-shaped way of an old-fashioned grandmother, but in the style of one whose only concessions to age are white hair and crow's feet, and whose figure and air are those of an active, up-to-date woman.

The second photograph was of two tall young men in uniform, one of them with the silvery blondness and golden

166

tan of someone of Nordic stock, and the other black-haired and teak-brown, with the amused hazel eyes which, only a short time ago, had been smiling into hers as the mature Joe said, 'Are you serious? There's only one thing I want—you, my lovely.'

She spent a long time studying this picture of him and his fellow *legionario*. Both were wearing scarlet-braided forage caps with scarlet tassels dangling above their right eyebrows, but whereas the sleeves of his companion's green tunic were unadorned, Joe had an extra touch of scarlet in the chevrons just above his cuffs. She did not know what rank this signified, but clearly the photograph had been taken when he had been in the Legion for some time and was aged at least nineteen or twenty.

In the years between then and now, life had honed away the traces of boyishness still visible at the time of the photograph; but even then it had been a face to remember, with a resolute look about the mouth and a glint of devilry in the eyes.

His grandmother and his friend were, apparently, the only two people of whom he wished to be reminded. There was no picture of his parents, or of any past girl-friends.

On the bulkhead at the back of his bunk was a painting of a ship with the sharp bows and raked masts of a tea-clipper. Recessed at the foot of the bunk were a number of shelves for a mixed collection of books, most of them having something to do with the sea. Two titles which caught her eye were *The Care and Repair of Hulls* and *Navigation by Pocket Calculator*.

She noticed a book on marine paintings on the oversize shelf at the bottom, and took it out to glance through it. She already knew from her mother's library of art books that the best ones were very expensive, and noting the price of Joe's book from the inside of the jacket, she wondered how he could have afforded it. Then she saw that the book had been a present. On the fly-leaf was written *With my thanks for ten heavenly days. Helen* and, below, the date of the inscription. The book had been given or sent to him more than two years ago. Without looking at the illustrations, Bianca closed the volume and replaced it.

She rose and smoothed the bunk's neat linen cover where she had sat for a few moments. Even here, in his private quarters, there was very little left about. A torch hung between spring clips within reach of his hand in the night. A zip-fastened leather writing case lay on the counter, and on a peg hung a striped bath-cum-lounging robe of dark blue terry towelling striped with bands of emerald velvet pile. An expensive robe not in keeping with Joe's simple life style and, by the look of it, seldom worn. Another present from Helen?

Half-ashamed of her curiosity, Bianca took it down and looked at the tag sewn at the back of the collar. As she had expected from the look of the garment, the label was that of one of the most exclusive men's shops in Jermyn Street. Undoubtedly a present from Helen.

Had she been here, in this cabin? Had Joe made love to her here? During those 'ten heavenly days' had she been playing truant from her marriage to the older man who had left her a wealthy widow?

Hating the jealousy which seethed in her—an emotion she had always despised—Bianca hurried from the cabin and went on deck.

It was not yet sunset, but the sun as it sank towards the mountains in the west had lost its fierce noonday glare. Many people were strolling about the harbour, nearly all of them in pairs.

A streak of gold, high up in the roseate sky, reminded

her that, if Joe had caught his plane, he would now be somewhere up there, but perhaps not thinking of her, as she was of him, but of the woman awaiting him in the south.

'Good evening, Bianca.'

She turned with a start to find Rufus standing on the quay behind her.

'Oh ... good evening. How are you?'

He had not resumed work on his memoirs following his illness, and although she had continued to visit him sometimes, it was nearly a week since her last call.

'I feel very well. Had two dips today. Don't swim yet, you know—just gently float for the time being. Now I'm off for my evening pre-prandial to the end of the sea-wall and back.'

'May I come with you?' she asked.

'With pleasure, my dear. Where's Joe? It's his night off, isn't it?'

'Yes, but he's been called away. I'll lock up. I shan't be a minute.'

As they stepped out along the quay together, she told Rufus what had occurred.

'Hmph, rather odd. *Very* odd,' was his comment when, in answer to his question, she had to admit that she did not yet know why Joe had had to leave so precipitately. 'In that case, why not come and have supper with me before you go home? You'll take a taxi, I hope. I don't hold with young women hitch-hiking. Never know what might happen to you, accepting a lift from a stranger. A Spaniard might make advances, and even if it was some Ancient Brit like myself, he might be in his cups and land you both in a ditch. No, you must take a taxi, my dear.'

'Yes, I should have done—had I been going home.'

She told him about Lucy and Ben, and that the Casa Mimosa would soon be for sale.

Impelled by a need to confide, she went on, 'I know you won't approve, Rufus, but Joe and I have decided to ... to join forces. That is, we had, before this happened. Now I'm not sure what's going to happen.'

'I see,' he said, glancing at her. 'I have to admit I should have preferred to see the pair of you setting up home in the old-fashioned way, as man and wife. But perhaps it will come to that later. At all events, I'm sure you'll both be very happy ... very well suited.'

'Do you think so?' she sighed.

'Certain of it. Never met two young people who seemed more suited to each other.'

'I don't know. I love Joe very much, but I have a feeling that what happened today will change things between us. I ought not to discuss him behind his back, but he is so mysterious, Rufus. I don't know where he was born, or where he grew up, or any of the things which most people usually mention quite early on. Sometimes it worries me a little.'

Rufus thought before he replied. Then, nodding his head, he said, 'Yes, to use a modern idiom, Joe does keep his cards close to his chest. Like you, I've long been aware that his past life is something he seems to prefer to forget. But if it's ever crossed your mind that he might have a black past, a shady past—and among expatriates there are always likely to be one or two scoundrels who can't go back where they came from because the police would be waiting for them—I believe you may safely dismiss that possibility. Joe may have a dash of the devil in him, but a brave devil, not a mean one.'

They had, by this time, been to the end of the wall and back. As they went aboard *Pago Pago*, Rufus said, 'Our meal won't take long. I prepared the potatoes and onions before setting out for my stroll.'

'I don't want to deprive you of half your supper,' said Bianca, who was not at all hungry but wanted the distraction of his company.

'Don't worry about that. When I make a *tortilla*, I always make a large one, and keep half to have cold next day. You will only be eating tomorrow's elevenses which I daresay I shouldn't have anyway. No, there's no need for you to help, my dear. I shouldn't be mollycoddled, you know. 'Lead a normal life, but don't overdo things' was what that doctor fellow told me.'

For an hour or so, while they ate, and afterwards drank the China tea which Rufus preferred to coffee, he succeeded in taking her mind if not wholly off her trouble, at least partially off it.

But when she was back on board Joe's boat there was no relief from the feeling of having been abandoned. Listening to the radio was no help as it did not force her to pay attention as conversing with Rufus had, and she soon found her thoughts wandering away from the programme.

The bunks in the two other cabins were not made up, which made her decide to sleep in Joe's cabin, even if lying there alone instead of with him did exacerbate her misery.

Even if her mind had been at rest, she would have found it hard to sleep with all the unfamiliar night-noises of the harbour disturbing the stillness to which she was accustomed. At midnight, a boat left the harbour, perhaps setting out on a moonlit crossing to Ibiza. She was a sailing boat, but she left under power and her wash, as it reached *La Libertad*, made her rock like a cradle. As Bianca and Rufus were probably the only two people who had by that time retired, it could not be said that the departing boat's skipper lacked consideration for others. By the sound of it, at least two parties were in progress, and indeed by both Spanish and holidaymaking standards, the night was still young.

It was two in the morning before something like silence descended and even then, she discovered, a boat, like an old house, was given to creaks and other noises which would not disturb someone used to them, but which were enough to keep her tossing and turning until the sheet beneath her was so ruckled that she had to get up and re-make the bed.

At half past two she rose again and, taking the torch from its clips, made her way to the galley for a long drink of cold water from the refrigerator. Suddenly, standing there, sipping a second glass of water and looking out at the grove of masts and moon-silvered rigging which was the view to starboard, she saw something she had over-looked. Why should Joe need his passport for a flight within Spain?

The only circumstance which made a passport neces-sary for an internal journey was when one was staying at hotels, and it was held by the management until the bill had been paid. If Joe had been going to Mrs Russell, surely he would have stayed at her villa, or shared her hotel suite? Perhaps he was now outside Spain, and on a mission very different from the one which had been torturing Bianca.

Could it be that his unwillingness to marry was because he already had one ill-judged and broken marriage behind him? Could it be that he also had a child?—A child who was not in his custody, but whom he loved and for whom, in the event of its sudden, serious illness, he would desert anyone, even the girl in his life.

It was the first acceptable explanation which had occurred to her in all the long hours of pondering and worrying. Holding the ice-cold glass against her hot forehead, she racked her memory for all the things Joe had ever said about marriage. Had he ever said, categorically, that he had never been married? She could not remember.

While she did not like the idea of his having a former wife somewhere, it was not as bitter a pill as the thought of his having another mistress with a stronger claim than her own. But his love for a child he had fathered was perfectly acceptable to her.

Perhaps this was the reason he never spoke of his past: because the loss of his small son or daughter pained him.

She went back to bed and lay down with her head on the pillow where, last night, his head had rested.

'Oh, Joe, I love you ... I love you,' she whispered aloud.

But as she closed her eyes and thought that she might, at last, sleep, her new supposition was shattered as she recalled that the call had come from Marbella, from Mrs Russell. And was it likely, was it at all believable that Helen Russell was the intermediary between Joe and the mother of his child?

CHAPTER TEN

In spite of having slept for less than three hours, Bianca was up early the next morning. Her first act was to take a towel and go for a swim on the seaward side of the harbour wall. The water was clear and calm in the early sun, and it made her feel better than she had when she had woken up with a headache and eyelids which felt as if they had sand underneath them.

Next she walked into town for a fresh roll to eat with her breakfast, buying one for Rufus as well. He was up and about when she returned, but if he noticed that she looked less clear-eyed than usual, he made no remark.

Fred, who had accompanied her part of the way to the bakery before being distracted by one of the port's many cats which he frequently chased but never caught, seemed to accept his master's disappearance and her presence without any uneasiness.

While the coffee was percolating, Bianca washed out the crumpled sheets and the pillow-case. The pillow, damp from the tears she had shed in the night, she put out to air in the sun. It seemed an eternity till noon. How could she fill in the hours until Joe called—if he called? Surely he would not forget. Surely he must have some notion of the agony of uncertainty in which he had left her.

By eleven, when she returned from another swim, the sheets were bone-dry. She re-made the bed and locked up, then walked to El Delfin where she ordered a coffee and watched, from her seat on the terrace, the hands of the clock in the bar creep slowly round to midday.

It was half a minute to twelve when the telephone started to ring, and she braced herself for the disappointment of it being a call for someone else.

The waiter on duty behind the bar picked up the receiver. '*Diga!*'

He knew Bianca was expecting a call. After a moment, he said, '*Si ... Uno momento, por favor,*' and beckoned.

With an unsteady hand she took up the receiver and said into the mouthpiece, 'Bianca speaking.'

'I half expected to be given a message from you telling me to go to the devil.'

It was a good line. Joe might have been standing behind her, so close did his voice sound.

'It did cross my mind,' she replied.

'I'll bet it did. But I hope you'll believe that I really had no alternative but to leave you in the lurch last night. I only got on that plane by the skin of my teeth. A delay of even five minutes and I should have missed it, which, if things had gone badly, I should have regretted very much.'

'If things had gone badly?' she queried.

'With my grandfather after his collapse. Not that he's out of the wood yet, but his chances are better than yesterday. It wasn't until Helen told me the old boy had been stricken like Rufus that I realised I was ready to make my peace with him. You didn't imagine I'd leave you, as things stood between us, for anything less than a life-or-death emergency, did you?'

'I—I hoped not,' she answered huskily. 'How did Mrs Russell know about your grandfather? Does he live in Marbella?'

'No, in London, which is where I am now. Helen was notified because she's also his grandchild, and the only member of the family, other than my grandmother, with whom I have any contact. My grandmother's not supposed to have anything to do with me, so Helen has been our go-between. It's a rather complex situation which I'll explain when I see you. As I want to remain for some days I'm hoping you'll join me.' His voice, always deep, seemed to deepen. 'Believe me, coming away was the hardest thing I've ever had to do. How soon can you come to London? Today? Tomorrow?'

'But, Joe——' she began.

'Rufus will look after Fred. If it's the air fare which worries you, forget it. I'll take care of that.'

'But you have to pay back your own fare. I don't understand about Mrs Russell. You surely can't mean she's your *sister*?'

'No, no, my cousin—the daughter of one of my aunts.'

'Why didn't you say so?'

'We'll go into that when I see you. I'm going to ring off now and call you back in thirty minutes, which will give you time to fix your flight. Go to it, darling.'

Her protest was wasted. He had cut the connection, leaving her to wonder if he had really called her darling, or if she had imagined it. If he had, it was the first time and, because he was not a man who used endearments casually, she could not help wondering if having to leave her the night before might have been, to a lesser degree, as revealing for him as his disappearance during the hill fire had been for her.

Throughout her flight to London the following day, Bianca was in a fever of uncertainty about Joe's motives in urging her to join him, and the reasons why he had been at odds with his grandfather.

It was an immense relief to have her misapprehensions about Helen Russell conclusively routed, though she found it impossible to conceive why Joe should have wished to conceal his true relationship with the woman who had given Bianca so many uneasy hours.

Having only an overnight case with her, and nothing to declare, she was not delayed in the baggage hall. Joe was waiting for her when she emerged from Customs, his tall figure made momentarily unfamiliar by a well-cut light grey summer suit which, having left Spain without luggage, he must have bought since his arrival.

To her surprise and disappointment, he didn't embrace her, but said only, 'Hello, Bianca,' and took charge of her case.

'Is your grandfather still making a good recovery?' she enquired, somewhat cast down by this unemotional reception.

'Yes, at present he's doing very well, but that's largely because he's had a fright and it's quietened him down. It won't be long before he reverts to type, and whether the staff at the hospital will be able to keep him in order when that happens remains to be seen.'

'You said on the telephone that you'd made your peace with him. Why had you been at odds with each other?'

He looked down at her, and smiled slightly. 'Later I'll tell you that, and the story of my life, but first things first. There's something I want to ask you.'

Instead of continuing on their way out of the concourse, he steered her towards a row of benches on which, for the moment, nobody was sitting.

'Were you sorry when I was called away so abruptly?' he asked her, as they sat down.

'Of course. Weren't you?'

A casual observer would have noticed no change in his expression. But as they were sitting turned towards each other, their knees almost touching, Bianca was close enough to see the sudden blaze in his eyes, and to realise that although his greeting had been friendly rather than lover-like, the passion which had flared between them three days ago was still smouldering under the surface.

'For myself—yes, very,' he answered. 'It seemed damn-ably bad luck to be called away at that moment. But later, when I was in a ... calmer frame of mind, I began to see it in a different light. If you're honest, I think you'll admit that your own reaction was probably tinged with relief. You would have preferred a more conventional type of honeymoon.'

Bianca could not refute it without admitting her love for him, so she said nothing.

He went on, 'Coming over in the plane, with nothing to do but think, I realised that, for the first time in my life, someone else's happiness was as important to me as my own—more important. I've always been very fond of my grandmother, but not to the extent of doing what the old boy demanded, and she hoped, I should do with my life. But I find that, for you, suddenly I *want* to become a solid citizen. All the things which once didn't matter to me now seem important because they will make you happy. I'm asking you to marry me, Bianca. I love you. I want to say "This is my wife". Will you have me for your husband?'

This was what she had not dared to let herself hope ever since he had called her 'darling' on the telephone.

'Oh, Joe, need you ask?—Yes, *yes*, YES!' she answered, her voice rising from a whisper to a joyous exclamation.

He caught her against him and hugged her and, for the first time in his arms, Bianca sensed that he felt more than passion for her. Passion was part of this new feeling between them, but it wasn't the whole any more. They were friends now as well as lovers; individuals still but also, for ever, a pair; their separate pasts forged into one indivisible future by the strong bonds of heart and mind which made marriage the best of all relationships, richer than ordinary friendships, stronger than any blood tie.

When they drew apart, he rose and picked up her case, and took her by the hand. 'Come on, darling, if we're going to be married immediately there's a lot to be done.'

'How immediately?' she asked.

'Tomorrow, if possible. If not, the day after. First we'll go and have lunch with my grandmother, and this afternoon you can choose an engagement ring and a wedding dress.'

'I don't need an engagement ring, Joe. I'll have one one day, when you're rich, but for the time being I'm quite content with a wedding ring.'

He looked down at her, the corners of his mouth twitching slightly.

'Why are you smiling at me like that?' she asked.

He shook his head and wouldn't tell her.

'What part of London does your grandmother live in?' she asked, as they emerged from the airport buildings.

'Not too far from the Zoo.'

'Have you told her about me ... about us?'

'Only your name, and that I want to marry you. Naturally she's keenly impatient to meet you.'

As he spoke, he handed her case to a middle-aged man in a navy blue suit and cap whom Bianca had noticed approaching and had expected to walk past them.

'This is Lamb, my grandfather's driver, Bianca. I'm happy to tell you that Miss Dawson has just agreed to change her name to Crawford, Lamb.'

The chauffeur beamed and touched the peak of his hat. 'Good morning, miss. Congratulations, Mr Jonathan, and allow me to wish you every happiness, miss.'

'Thank you.' She turned to Joe. 'Is your name really Jonathan?'

'Jonathan Julius Alexander Birkdale Crawford, but I'm always called Joe by my family.'

That his grandfather had a chauffeur had surprised her. When she saw him open the rear door of a huge silver-grey Rolls-Royce she was stunned. She had judged that Joe had a prosperous middle-class background, but had never imagined that his grandparents had an income of the order required to run this magnificent car.

As she sank on to the luxurious upholstery and Lamb closed the door and went to put her cheap chain-store suitcase in a boot which could no doubt accommodate a matched set of Vuitton luggage, she remember Joe's enigmatic look when she had said she did not need an engagement ring.

'Are you rich already?' she asked him.

'Not as rich as my grandfather, but my father left me fairly well heeled. Not that I've ever touched his money, because until recently I felt that I couldn't use Crawford money while rejecting all family claims on me. Now that I'm about to conform to the pattern set by my great-grandfather, it's no longer inconsistent to make use of my share of the family fortune.'

Lamb had taken his place behind the wheel, but he could not hear their conversation through the panel of thick glass which separated the front of the car from the spacious back part.

'I said I'd tell you my life story and, very briefly, I will so that you aren't quite in the dark when you meet my grandmother,' Joe went on.

'My great-grandfather was and my grandfather still is an immensely forceful character. In many ways, a tyrant. My father, his only son, was not a strong personality. My

mother married him for money, and they led a cat-and-dog
life until, when I was nine, she ditched him for an even
richer American. Father died when I was thirteen. My
parents' endless rows had made me indifferent to them
both, and also I despised my father for letting himself be
forced into the family firm when he would have preferred
to study medicine. So when my grandfather began to lay
out my future for me, I told him I had different ideas. He
was furious—to put it mildly—and told me he never wanted
to see me again, and forbade my grandmother to have any
contact with me.'

'Has she never stood up to him?' asked Bianca.

'No. She's not by nature a doormat, but she loves him,
and she accepts that the only method of living peacefully
with him is to let him have his way in all things. I believe
it upset her to cut me out of her life, but she's always
been totally loyal to Grandfather even when she doesn't
agree with him. She wouldn't write to me, or let me write
to her, because he'd expressly forbidden it; but we have
exchanged verbal messages sometimes through Helen.'

'When you introduced me to Mrs Russell, why didn't
you say she was your cousin?' Bianca asked.

'I suppose because, even then, I didn't want you to
associate me with her life style,' he said reflectively. 'A long
time ago I resolved that if I did ever marry, which then
seemed unlikely, I should have to be absolutely certain
that my wife didn't give a damn for position or money. I
wanted a girl who would throw in her lot with me if I
chose to spend the rest of my life playing wallpaper music
or chartering. And I found one,' he added, raising her
hand, which he had been holding all the time they had
been in the car, and brushing her knuckles with his lips.

'Talking of wallpaper music, I propose to go back to
Spain and continue playing at El Delfin until the end

of the season or until Piet can replace me, whichever is the sooner. Then we'll come back to London and set up home, and I'll start learning all the things I shall need to know if I'm to take over from my grandfather one of these days. But that won't be for several years yet. The old boy has had a close shave, but he isn't finished by any means.'

'He sounds rather frightening,' she said. 'Does he know about you and me?'

'Not yet. I may tell him tonight. At present he's allowed only two visitors a day—my grandmother and me. It will be a little while yet before you have to beard the old lion.' He released her hand, but only to slip his arm round her and pull her against him. 'And he won't roar at you, my lovely.'

'What sort of business is it that you will eventually take over?' she asked.

'Crawfords are City of London shipbrokers, and the fourth largest privately owned company in Britain,' he explained. 'They also own the Anchor Line of bulk grain tankers. My grandfather is the chairman of both boards, but I shall have to start on the ground floor.'

In describing his grandparents' home as 'not far from the Zoo', he had meant, she discovered, that they lived in Chester Terrace, one of the famous Nash terraces by Regent's Park.

His grandmother was waiting for them in the forty-foot drawing-room on the first floor. She took Bianca's hand in hers. 'I'm delighted to meet you at last. I heard about you some time ago from my granddaughter Helen, who, as I think you know, is a great admirer of your mother's beautiful paintings. She said you were a charming girl, and if Joe has fallen in love with you, I know your nature must match your looks. I knew as soon as he arrived that something important had happened to him, and it makes me immensely happy to see him looking so happy.'

'You don't yet know that she has accepted me,' said her grandson.

'I knew it the instant I watched you get out of the car, my dear. Love is a condition instantly recognisable to those who have ever been in it, and although it's nearly fifty years ago, I haven't forgotten the glow of my own engagement to your grandfather. Even he walked on air for a time,' she added, with a twinkle. She turned to Bianca again. 'It's a wonderful phase of one's life when love bursts into bloom and the everyday world becomes paradise. Now tell me your plans. It goes without saying that Joe is far too impatient to wait while we arrange a formal wedding. It wouldn't surprise me to learn he already has a licence in his pocket.'

'Have you?' Bianca asked him.

'No, because after leaving you so abruptly I wasn't sure you would have me—or at least, not immediately,' he answered, with a provoking glint in his eyes.

After lunch he took her to Bond Street where he bought her a beautiful one-carat diamond, a solitaire on a band of platinum to match a plain platinum wedding ring.

'Off you go to choose your dress while I attend to the formalities,' he told her, outside the jeweller's. 'I'll meet you for tea at Claridges at half past four.'

Earlier Bianca had wanted to go to her bank in Kensington and cash a cheque, but Joe had dismissed this suggestion as unnecessary, and had insisted on giving her more crisp new twenty-pound notes than she had ever carried on her before.

When they separated, she walked along Bond Street with her shoulder bag tucked securely under her left elbow, and the diamond catching the sunlight and flashing white fire.

There was a designer whose clothes she had always admired but had never felt she could afford; but when she met Joe for tea she was laden with carriers containing wedding clothes by Shuji Tojo.

'I hope you'll approve,' she said, as he relieved her of her parcels. 'I've been wildly extravagant, but at least I haven't bought the kind of dress—in fact not a dress at all—which is only good for one occasion. These things will be wearable for ages, perhaps not immediately but later, when we're living here.'

'I want you to be extravagant. Anything you want, I want you to have,' he told her, as they went into the green and grey lounge and found a fairly secluded corner.

Presently Joe amused her by showing a schoolboyish relish for smoked salmon sandwiches, millefeuilles and custard tarts topped with grapes. To please him, she ate one sandwich and one of the delicious tarts, but being in a state of exalted happiness seemed to have taken away her appetite. She still could not quite believe that all this was really happening. It still had a dream like quality.

When they went back to Chester Terrace they found Lady Crawford had been to see her husband and had told him of Joe's engagement. He wanted to see Bianca for himself and, knowing his temperament, his doctor had agreed that she should accompany Joe when he visited his grandfather that evening.

In spite of Joe's reassurances, Bianca rather dreaded her presentation to the despotic old man who, for so many years, had cut Joe out of his life because he would not be bullied.

When she met him, she found it hard to believe that Sir John was seventy-five and, only a few days before, had been rushed to hospital. He was an older version of Joe, with thick white hair instead of thick dark hair, and a fierce blue gaze instead of Joe's amused hazel eyes.

'So you're the young woman who has finally persuaded my grandson to give up all this footloose nonsense and become a respectable member of society,' was his first remark, before Joe could introduce her.

'No, that isn't quite right,' she said mildly. 'I hope I shall never persuade Joe to do anything he doesn't wish to do. If he wants to continue being footloose, I shall be glad to go with him. If he chooses to become "respectable", I'll settle for that equally happily. I don't mind where or how we live, as long as I'm with him.'

The old man glowered for a moment. 'Silly girl is head over heels in love with you,' he remarked, addressing his grandson. 'Hoped she might be a sensible person.'

'No less sensible than Grandmother, who has always done exactly as you wanted,' Joe remarked dryly. 'Did you hope I would marry one of those liberated females who refuse to be Mrs Anyone, and sign themselves M-stroke-S?'

'Certainly not! Never heard such tomfool nonsense. Had you picked one of those arrogant creatures, you wouldn't have had *my* blessing, I can assure you. A woman may be as clever as she likes, and if she chooses to become an engineer rather than a housewife, or a scientist rather than a mother, I say nothing in opposition to that. But let her also be feminine; not one of these modern viragos who seem to regard men as enemies.'

'They have been our enemies at times; but I think, for my generation, the sex war is over and peace has broken out,' said Bianca. 'And as far as I'm personally concerned, I can't wait to stop being Miss Dawson and start being Mrs Jonathan Crawford.'

They did not stay long with Sir John, but before they left he expressed regret that he could not be present at their marriage the following day, and said he looked forward to another visit from them afterwards, before they flew back to Spain.

From the hospital they went to the theatre, and then to Cecconi's for an Italian supper beginning with home-made pasta with a golden topping of cheese direct from the grill, then a beef *carpaccio*, and finally a dish of fresh figs.

'Shall we go and say goodnight to my grandmother? She goes to bed early but reads late,' said Joe, when a taxi dropped them outside the house.

Lady Crawford put down her book as they entered the pretty bedroom where she was leaning against a mound of pale pink pillows in a four-poster bed curtained with white glazed chintz lined with rose-coloured taffeta.

'Was the play good?' she asked, smiling at them.

Between them, sitting on the edge of her bed with Bianca leaning lightly against Joe's shoulder and his arms loosely linked around her, they described the evening.

The three of them talked until nearly midnight, when Lady Crawford said, 'I think I should send you to bed now. You have a long day ahead of you.'

They said goodnight to her, and walked together along the thickly carpeted landing to the door of the equally pretty bedroom which Bianca had been given. In the darkness of the back of the taxi, Joe had taken her in an ardent embrace, his hands warmly caressing the softness of her yielding body. Now she wondered if he would think it a nonsense to postpone the fulfilment of their hunger for each other's arms until tomorrow. If, having opened her door for her, he had entered the bedroom, intending to stay, she would not have objected.

But he chose instead to put a hand under her chin and kiss her lightly on the forehead. 'Sleep tight,' he said, rather huskily. Then he withdrew, and the door closed quietly behind him.

She had been told that breakfast would be brought to her in bed and, next morning, on the tray were two presents for her.

Lady Crawford's gift was a pair of antique emerald drop earrings, with a note—*These were given to his bride by my husband's grandfather, and it has become a tradition that they should be passed down to each Crawford bride on her wedding day. I can't tell you how glad it makes me that this happy occasion has come about much sooner than any of us expected.*

The second small package contained a pair of modern diamond-studded butterfly pins. On the card in the satin-lined box, Joe had drawn a heart enclosing their initials and the date, and Bianca knew that, for sentimental reasons, she would treasure the slip of pasteboard as much as the jewels for her ears.

She and her bridegroom went to their civil wedding accompanied by their two witnesses, his grandmother and his cousin Helen, who had arrived in England late the night before.

Both women were obviously sincere in their praise for Bianca's unconventional wedding clothes, which consisted of a crêpe-de-chine blouse with a skirt of a heavier silk and close-fitting quilted crêpe-de-chine jacket, all in shades of the sea-green colour which went so well with her honey-brown Spanish tan.

A hat which perched on her forehead and had a small nose-tip veil, and a pair of high-heeled kid shoes, completed her outfit. In place of the usual spray, Joe had realised from what she had told him that this would not do, and had been out early to find her one perfect rose with a long stem and creamy-white petals beginning to open.

Within ten hours of her wedding the rose, with its stem cut short, was pinned to the collar of a dress more suitable for travelling, and she and Joe were back in Spain.

His first call was to El Delfin to tell Piet he would be back at the piano the next day, and to repay the money the Dutchman had lent him. Then they called on Rufus, to announce their marriage and collect Fred.

The moon was rising above the port when *La Libertad* left her moorings and quitted the harbour, heading south. Before the moon had fully risen, she was lying in a bay where no other craft rode the silver sea, and the nearest people were up in the cliff top villas scattered along the wooded coastline.

'Alone at last!' said Joe, smiling when, having made sure the boat was secure on her anchorage, he stepped down into the cockpit and took Bianca in his arms.

She slid her arms round his neck, closing her eyes against the moonlight.

'It's been such a lovely day, Joe. I'm so happy,' she murmured, sighing.

His strong arms tightened around her. His lips were warm on her cheek.

'Now for the night, *vida mia.*'

Harlequin Plus
A VOICE FROM THE PAST

Anne Weale's hero, Joe, is fond of quoting Renaissance poetry to Bianca. Robert Herrick (1591-1674) appears to be one of his favorite poets, and the following poem is particularly appropriate to Joe's and Bianca's circumstances. It's called "To the Virgins, to make much of Time."

Gather ye Rose-buds while ye may,
    Old Time is still a flying:
And this same flower that smiles to day,
    To morrow will be dying.

The glorious Lamp of Heaven, the Sun,
    The higher he's a getting;
The sooner will his Race be run,
    And neerer he's to Setting.

That Age is best, which is the first,
    When Youth and Blood are warmer;
But being spent, the worse, and worst
    Times, still succeed the former.

Then be not coy, but use your time;
    And well ye may, goe marry;
For having lost but once your prime,
    You may for ever tarry.

Take these 4 best-selling novels FREE

That's right! FOUR first-rate Harlequin romance novels by four world renowned authors, FREE, as your introduction to the Harlequin Presents Subscription Plan. Be swept along by these FOUR exciting, poignant and sophisticated novels . . . .
Travel to the Mediterranean island of Cyprus in **Anne Hampson**'s "Gates of Steel" . . . to Portugal for **Anne Mather**'s "Sweet Revenge" . . . to France and **Violet Winspear**'s "Devil in a Silver Room" . . . and the sprawling state of Texas for **Janet Dailey**'s "No Quarter Asked."

Harlequin Presents...

The very finest in romantic fiction

Join the millions of avid Harlequin readers all over the world who delight in the magic of a really exciting novel. EIGHT great NEW titles published EACH MONTH!
Each month you will get to know exciting, interesting, true-to-life people . . . . You'll be swept to distant lands you'v dreamed of visiting . . . . Intrigue, adventure, romance, and the destiny of many lives will thrill you through each Harlequin Presents novel.

Get all the latest books before they're sold out!
As a Harlequin subscriber you actually receive your personal copies of the latest Presents novels immediately after they come off the press, so you're sure of getting all 8 each month.

Cancel your subscription whenever you wish!
You don't have to buy any minimum number of books. Whenever you decide to stop your subscription just let us know and we'll cancel all further shipments.